CURSES & CLIFFHANGERS

A LIBRARY WITCH MYSTERY

ELLE ADAMS

.

To be notified when Elle Adams's next book is released, sign up to her author newsletter.

D ating the Reaper came with its fair share of
pitfalls.

The attention we drew wasn't one of them,
though it could get annoying when people insisted on
staring at the pair of us whenever we went anywhere
together.

In fairness, in their place, I might have stared too,
since Xavier was gorgeous in a way which was frankly
inhuman. Ironic, considering he *wasn't* human, and while
he could have made himself invisible if he liked, I'd have
drawn even more attention if I'd been sitting alone at a
table in the Black Dog, eating ice cream and talking to
myself.

"Anyway, I think Aunt Adelaide has regrets about
putting Aunt Candace in charge of the front desk yesterday," I said to Xavier. "She was paying so little attention
that two kids tried to take a book of practical jokes out of
the library without checking it out. Instead of chasing

them down like a normal person, she pushed them into the vampire's basement."

The blond Reaper grinned. "I bet that'll guarantee they won't forget again."

"There was a lot of shrieking involved." The vampire in question hadn't woken up in decades, and nobody entirely knew how he'd ended up there in the first place, but I'd had a couple of unintended visits to his basement before, and I couldn't say they'd been particularly enjoyable. "I decided not to tell Estelle. She has her hands full with her thesis, and I know she feels bad about leaving the rest of us to pick up the slack. She doesn't need to hear about Aunt Candace making a nuisance of herself."

"At least she was quick on the uptake," he remarked. "I know she's not exactly the most observant of people."

"You're telling me. She's supposed to be in charge of my magic lessons, and it's nearly impossible to get her to stay on topic."

A few giggles drew my attention to the nearby table, where several teenage girls were watching us with wistful expressions on their faces. I assumed they were at the age where the idea of dating a Reaper seemed romantic and not terrifying, though there was nothing remotely terrifying about Xavier. Regardless, I had the occasional urge to pinch myself every so often to remind myself our relationship was real.

Xavier's aquamarine gaze flickered in their direction for a moment before he returned his attention to me. The stares didn't seem to bother him, though it took little to faze someone whose job involved escorting departed souls to the world beyond and who carried an invisible scythe strapped to his back for that very purpose. Teenage girls were hardly a threat, not compared to his boss, the Grim Reaper.

Yes… *that* Grim Reaper. Let's just say it'd been a battle and a half to get him to accept I was dating his apprentice, since Reapers weren't supposed to form attachments to regular people. Supposedly it interfered with their ability to do their jobs. I was more inclined to think his job interfered with his ability to pursue a relationship with me, since I could count the number of uninterrupted dates we'd had in the last few months on one hand.

Xavier called the waiter over to fetch the bill while the teenagers seemed to realise we'd noticed their staring and hastily turned back to their own table. As usual, Xavier insisted on paying for both of us. Where he got his money, I wasn't entirely sure, given that the Grim Reaper wasn't exactly the typical kind of employer. Regardless, he always seemed to have cash on hand, so I didn't voice an argument. Relieved to get away from the giggling teenagers, I let him pay and turned to leave the pub.

I slid my hand into his as we walked out into the cold evening air while the girls swooned and sighed behind us. "I wouldn't have blamed you if you'd turned yourself invisible back then."

"That wouldn't have been nearly as fun," he said.

"Why?" I asked. "It can't be fun being stared at, either."

Reapers had the handy ability to hide in the shadows wherever they wanted to, but Xavier's confidence in keeping our relationship out in the open warmed me more efficiently than his hand in mine as we walked through the chilly night air.

"Sometimes I get bored hiding in the shadows." His

fingers stroked my palm. "It'd also mean I didn't get to look at you."

My stomach swooped downward. "Well, we can't have that, can we?"

He bent his head to kiss me and then stiffened midmotion. "Ah... one second."

"Let me guess." I dropped his hand. "Your boss is calling you?"

"To escort a soul to the afterlife, yes."

Typical. Instead of texting or calling like a normal person, the Grim Reaper used some kind of unseen magic to call his apprentice to his side, wherever he happened to be. "In other words, someone died."

And it'd all been going so well.

"I'll walk you back to the library first," he said. "The body isn't far from here, but I can't imagine my boss will want me to bring you to the scene of the crime."

My heart dropped. "You mean it was murder?"

"When a body is found in an open location, I tend to assume there's a fair chance it was murder," he said. "We'd better go."

If nothing else, at least we'd got through the 'date' portion of the evening without an interruption. We made our way across the seafront and headed up the street which ran alongside the clock tower towards the town square. My family's library dominated the square, an impressive brick construction five storeys high which towered over its neighbours. Working in a magical library was almost as demanding as Xavier's position as Reaper, especially when I was still learning to use biblio-witch magic—my family's speciality, which enabled us to draw magic from the written word. In between helping my best friend Laney adjust to being a vampire and running errands for my family, it was a miracle I found any time for a romantic life at all.

Xavier and I came to an abrupt halt when the Grim Reaper stepped out of the shadows like a piece of the night sky in the form of a hooded figure wielding a sharp scythe. Whether he'd ever been human, none of us knew. Except Xavier, of course, but I'd never probed him for more details despite my Aunt Candace's endless questions on the subject.

My heart gave an unpleasant lurch. "The person who died isn't near the library, are they?"

Instead of answering, the Grim Reaper addressed his apprentice. "I told you not to neglect your job."

"I wasn't neglecting anything," Xavier replied. "I was escorting Rory home to the library before I came to find you. I didn't think you'd appreciate it if I brought her to the scene of the crime."

"You should have come to me right away."

"You think he should have simply vanished and left me standing there?" The answer, no doubt, was 'yes'. Typical of the Grim Reaper, who had zero understanding of human relationships.

Once again, the Grim Reaper ignored me, instead beckoning for Xavier to follow him. I might as well not have even existed. A jolt of annoyance travelled up my spine, and before I could question the wisdom of ticking him off, I fell into step with Xavier and followed the Grim Reaper across the square.

Xavier's brows shot up. "Rory...?"

"If he's going to interrupt our date, then I'd like to

know why." Besides, if someone had been murdered near the library, then maybe I knew who they were.

The Grim Reaper came to a halt at the end of an alleyway, where the body of a redheaded wizard lay sprawled on his back. Not someone I recognised, but given the location, it was better to be safe than sorry.

"His soul has already gone?" Xavier asked his boss.

"Yes, I guided him to the afterlife myself."

Xavier studied the Grim Reaper's shadowy form. "You didn't need me to come here, then, did you?"

No. He just wanted to ruin our night. For someone who might have been hundreds of years old for all I knew, the Grim Reaper could certainly be as vindictive as a regular person. While part of me was tempted to call him out on it, I didn't quite trust him not to use his scythe on me if I did, so I settled for glowering at him. Which he ignored.

Xavier returned to my side, and I whispered, "Xavier, do you know how he died?"

"No idea, but there's no visible wounds on him," he said. "Weird. If I'd spoken to his ghost, I might have asked…"

The Grim Reaper glided between us, bringing a chill which froze the blood in my veins. "What are you still doing here, Aurora Hawthorn?"

At least he'd finally acknowledged my existence. "You didn't tell me to leave. Besides, someone has to report this wizard's death to the police."

"I'll call Edwin," said Xavier, referring to the local head of the police force.

"That won't be necessary," said the Grim Reaper.

Seriously? If you asked me, he was trying to ensure the two of us didn't spend any longer together than he deemed suitable—but leaving the poor wizard in an alleyway overnight was petty beyond belief.

Xavier pulled out his phone. "He might have died of natural causes, but someone needs to be told."

"Put that thing away." The Grim Reaper gave the phone in Xavier's hand such a withering look that you'd think it'd mortally insulted him. Xavier had had to fight a battle with him to get a mobile phone in the first place, as a way of staying in contact with me. With a sixth sense connecting the two of them at all times, the Grim Reaper didn't need access to a phone or to the internet to be able to bother his apprentice at any given time.

Luckily—or not—a passing group of witches came tottering past on high heels at that moment.

"Hey… it's the Reaper!" One of them nearly tripped over her own feet in an effort to get a close look at Xavier and then *did* trip when the Grim Reaper emerged from the shadows in front of their group. As she landed on her rear, the other two witches spotted the body lying in the alleyway behind us.

Several loud shrieks ensued while I wished I'd had the good sense to hightail it back to the library before I'd been caught next to a dead body in public *again.*

Xavier leaned in to whisper, "I'd go back to the library. They're already calling the police, and it's probably better if Edwin didn't find you here."

I dipped my head. "Will you let me know if you figure out how he died?"

"Sure." He cast a guilty look in the direction of his boss, who stood nearby, an imposing shadow condemning us for daring to defy him. "I'll see you later."

"Tomorrow." I planted a brief kiss on his lips before

turning away, the sound of the three witches' shrieking echoing across the square as I walked.

My mood deteriorated the closer I got to the library. Not because of the dead body—it was hardly the poor wizard's fault he'd died—but because the Grim Reaper's efforts to drive a wedge between Xavier and me had crossed a line between annoying and downright disruptive. He was forever dragging Xavier away on 'Reaper business', and I knew for a fact there weren't *that* many deaths for him to handle, considering Ivory Beach was a small town and the Reaper's territory didn't cover much land outside of it.

No, he just wanted an excuse to keep us apart from one another, and I didn't care for it a bit. While Xavier had given me a magical stone with which I could draw him to my side at any moment, I was only supposed to use it in emergencies. This situation, however annoying it might be, did not count as an emergency, so the most I could do was send him a text message and hope that the library's notoriously unpredictable signal was cooperating tonight.

Entering the library, I crossed the darkened entryway to the corridor leading to our family's living quarters. While the main part of the library was lit by floating lanterns at night which cast a warm yellow light over the shelves, the living quarters remained shadowed. Consequently, I nearly walked into my cousin, Cass, on my way in.

"You don't look happy," she remarked. "I take it your date didn't go as planned?"

"Ooh, trouble in paradise?" Sylvester predictably

popped up, the huge tawny owl perching on top of one of Aunt Adelaide's store cupboards.

"No," I said. "The Grim Reaper decided to drag Xavier away to see to a dead body, even though the departed soul had already been banished."

"Who bit the dust this time?" Sylvester asked.

"A local wizard," I said. "Don't look at me like that, Cass. Someone else called the police, so I figured I'd be better off coming back here before we all got dragged in for questioning. It's not like I saw how he died."

Neither had Xavier, for that matter.

"Are you sure the Grim Reaper didn't set you up?" Cass sounded entirely too amused at the possibility. "If he's taken to sticking his scythe in random passers-by to stop you and Xavier from dating, you must really have got under his skin. Well done."

"Don't be absurd," I said while Sylvester cackled in the background. "I'm pretty sure it's against one of his all-important Reaper rules to take someone's soul if the person isn't already dead. He's just being obnoxious."

"Isn't that part of the Grim Reaper's job description?" Cass snorted. "If you expect him to behave otherwise, you might as well tell Aunt Candace to give up novel writing."

"*What* did you just say?" Aunt Candace herself walked into the room from the kitchen, a pile of books tucked under her arm. Her auburn hair was as wild as ever, flowing free where Cass's was tied back neatly.

"She was comparing you to the Grim Reaper," Sylvester said.

"He's lying," Cass told her aunt. "I was saying the Grim Reaper is as inclined to be a grump as you're inclined to be writing a book. Which is true."

"She's a grump, too, precaffeine," said the owl.

That, I could agree with. "Forget the Reaper. I'm going to get an early night."

"So you're giving up?" Cass said. "You're going to let the Grim Reaper win?"

"Pretty sure he always wins, considering the whole scythe thing."

That made Sylvester snicker, but Cass merely rolled her eyes. "You know that's not what I'm talking about. How many times has he cut your date nights short now?"

"There's nothing I can do to stop the Grim Reaper from dragging his apprentice away if someone's dead," I said. "They're connected via some kind of psychic link, so it's not like he can switch off his phone."

"Creepy," said Cass. "Yes, I know that's in the job description too. Maybe you can try to distract him."

"Nothing distracts the Grim Reaper," I said. "He exists for two things—reaping souls and training his apprentice to do the same."

"Does Xavier even need any more training?" Cass asked. "I doubt it. Would throwing a soul in his path distract him?"

"Where would you get the soul?" I frowned at her. "If you want me to commit murder to get a date, then I'm out."

Aunt Candace cackled. "If you do, please let me know so I can borrow the storyline for a book and interview you while you're in jail."

"Nobody's going to jail," Cass said. "You can work out the logistics with Xavier, can't you? Surely there's a way to... I don't know, send a soul to lead him on a wild ghost chase for a bit."

"I really don't think there is," I said. "The Grim Reaper wouldn't let a simple lost soul get the better of him, and I'd be in real trouble if he found out I was responsible."

While the Reapers weren't supposed to take the souls of anyone who wasn't dead, anyone who angered them was fair game. I'd prefer not to learn what it felt like to end up on the pointy end of a scythe.

She shrugged. "Your choice."

"I can distract him," said Sylvester.

"No, thanks." The owl didn't *have* a soul to reap, or at least I assumed he didn't, being the embodiment of the library's entire store of knowledge who everyone thought was simply a harmless familiar who'd been put under a permanent talking spell. Why he preferred to spend his time chasing late fees and winding me up, I hadn't the faintest idea, but he and Cass were a nightmare to deal with on most days, let alone at the tail end of the frustrating evening I'd already had.

I left them to their scheming and retreated to my room instead of listening to more ill-advised suggestions from the pair of them. I'd come up with another strategy for getting around the Grim Reaper in the morning.

2

The following morning, I sat behind the front desk in the library as we prepared to open for the day. Estelle, my cousin and Cass's sister, smiled at me as she walked past with a stack of books in her arms.

"Are you okay watching the front desk today, Rory?" Estelle adjusted her grip on the teetering pile of books. "I'd volunteer, but I have to work on my thesis."

"No worries," I said. "I'd rather keep the general public safe from Aunt Candace throwing anyone into the vampire's basement again. How's it going?"

"Slow." She shuffled along with the books balanced in her arms while Spark, the pixie, flew along behind her. "Very slow. I understand why Aunt Candace gives you that dead-eyed stare when you ask her how it's going at a certain point in the manuscript."

"At least you only have to do it once, right?" Estelle had been working on her magical PhD in her spare time for the last few years, but her thesis would be the culmination of all her efforts.

"Assuming I ever reach the end." Estelle sighed when one of the books fell off the pile, which Spark, the pixie, retrieved for her with a chirp of encouragement.

"You will," I encouraged her. "Just remember to sleep."

She yawned. "I also understand why Aunt Candace always says she gets her best ideas at night."

"It's Laney who's supposed to be active at night, remember?" I'd already figured she'd had a few late nights given how her eyes were underscored with dark shadows, and her curly auburn hair was as wild as Aunt Candace's. "Next you'll be guzzling coffee and making yourself a research cave like Aunt Candace."

She shot me a tired grin. "The room I'm working in is starting to resemble Aunt Candace's, I'll admit. I'll let you know if I get the sudden impulse to start writing under a secret pen name."

"As long as you refrain from getting locked in jail in order to question the local police, you're probably fine."

She snorted. "Oh, and we have the poetry night this evening as well. Can you knock on my door as a reminder if I forget? I barely know what time it is these days."

"Sure." I made a mental note to pick up some food from Zee's bakery to drop off at her room, too, given her recent tendency to forget to eat. "Good luck."

Estelle departed while I sat behind the front desk and pulled out the leather-bound journal which had belonged to my dad before his death. I'd spent the last few weeks making frustratingly slow progress with translating his journal entries into English from some kind of bizarre code my dad had made up himself and which I'd had to use a specially made translator spell to decipher. Even after running the whole journal through the translator spell, I had to go through each page one at a time, so it was taking me a while to assemble the pages into some kind of coherent order.

Typically, as soon as I opened the journal, Sylvester swooped over and landed on the desk. Suppressing a sigh, I lifted my head. "What is it?"

"Don't let me interrupt you," he said, pointing at the journal with his beak. "Go on."

"You're literally sitting on the document, Sylvester." The notoriously mischief-prone owl always seemed to know when I wanted some peace and quiet, and I found it impossible to focus when he was hovering over my shoulder. No wonder I had yet to unearth any answers from the journal concerning my dad's history with the vampires.

Judging by what I'd read so far, I'd been a small child when he'd written these journal entries, and I'd had no clue at all that he'd ever been part of a hidden magical world which existed alongside the regular mundane one. The rest of my family had assumed he'd left his old life behind when he'd decided to marry my mum and have me, and he had renounced the magical world until his death a few years prior, but the journal said otherwise. He might have given up his wand, but whatever the journal contained had drawn the attention of a group of deadly vampires known as the Founders.

Eventually, they'd come looking for me as well. Even moving to Ivory Beach hadn't spared me from their desperate attempts to snag the journal for their own, and my most recent encounter with them had seen my best friend transformed into a vamp herself. For that reason, looking at the journal stirred up a complex mix of emotions, and most of my family was happy to leave me to uncover the answers on my own.

Except, of course, for a certain owl. "I don't see the need for secrecy."

"You eat mice, Sylvester. You and I don't see eye to eye on a lot of things."

The owl made a clucking noise with his beak and then took off as the library's door opened and several people walked in. Most were regulars here—some students from the university studying for their dissertations or working on assignments—who were pretty self-sufficient most of the time. That worked in my favour, since I could just point them to the Reading Corner while I worked on the journal, and I could still be available to answer their occasional queries. I'd become adept at multitasking, especially since Estelle's recent habit of staying in her room working on her thesis.

I hadn't heard from Xavier since the previous night, but that was to be expected given the trouble we both had getting a decent phone signal. I had no more reason than usual to suspect interference from the Grim Reaper, so I did my best to put the previous evening to the back of my mind and turned the page of the journal. At least that was progressing slightly faster than my relationship... which was kind of a depressing prospect.

Okay, maybe I hadn't entirely forgotten my annoyance at the Grim Reaper, but come on. I'd naively assumed that once he'd given us permission to date, we'd at least have a fifty-fifty chance of getting through a date night without him yanking Xavier away. As it was, our record was more like ten percent proper dates, ninety percent interruptions. Which was unfair on Xavier as well as me.

The moment I returned my attention to the page, Aunt Adelaide—Estelle and Cass's mother and the person who technically owned the library—crossed the lobby wearing her usual long black silver-lined cloak. Tall and curvy with red hair like the rest of us, she halted beside the desk and gave me a smile. "Everything okay? You don't mind watching the desk today, do you?"

"It's no problem," I said. "Are you heading out?"

"I've been asked to take a few books to the local hospital to help them identify the cause of the death of a local wizard," she said. "He was found last night in an alleyway on the other side of the square. Can you imagine?"

"Was he the body the Grim Reaper found?" My heart gave an uneasy flip. "Xavier and I ran into him on the way back from our date. I thought Cass might have told you."

"You know she doesn't tell me anything," said Aunt Adelaide. "Did the Grim Reaper mention anything about the cause of death? Or does he not pay attention to such things?"

"Unfortunately not," I said. "Who was the person who died?"

"His name was Rufus, but the police and doctors are baffled because there are no obvious signs of what caused his death," she said. "By all accounts, he simply dropped dead out of nowhere. Poisoning has been ruled out, so I'm going to offer them some of our best books on magical causes of death in the hopes that they can figure it out."

"I hope they do."

The Grim Reaper *hadn't* stuck his scythe in a random

guy just to get at Xavier, had he? That was a bit much even for him, but I couldn't think of any other magical means of causing someone to drop dead on the spot. Then again, my own expertise was limited given the relatively short time I'd spent in the magical world so far. If the town's doctors couldn't work out the cause of death, then surely the library ought to be able to point them in the right direction.

After my aunt departed, I returned my attention to the journal, groaning under my breath when I found yet another page where my dad had insisted on scribbling in the margins of his past journal entries and confusing the translator spell. Pulling out a notebook, I resigned myself to reassembling pieces of sentences like a particularly confusing jigsaw puzzle.

I shouldn't be surprised, since Dad's slapdash organisational habits had annoyed his friend and co-worker Abe to no end. It wouldn't have surprised me if he'd left a confusing trail for the vampires to follow entirely by accident, which at least explained why they hadn't caught up to him until years after his death. Unfortunately, it was causing me a serious headache at the moment to unearth *why* the vampires had been hell-bent on possessing the journal. So far, all I'd found was a long series of passages describing a trip to Europe he'd taken while I was a toddler, which had involved getting lost in a typical Dad fashion and ending up at the wrong airport.

The tale evoked an odd kind of nostalgia in me, and when I probed my memories, I did vaguely recall questioning Mum about his work trips. She'd claimed he'd gone to buy rare books for the shop, and as a kid, I hadn't questioned if there were any holes in that explanation. He and Abe had been joint owners of a small bookshop which barely turned a profit, and there was no *logical* reason for him to take so many field trips, but Abe had had zero connection to the paranormal world. Hence why he'd tried to throw away my dad's journal when I'd found it in the bookshop after his death. I'd taken it for myself instead and carried it everywhere out of sentimental value, or so I'd thought at the time.

I'd never have imagined anyone would be interested in its contents, much less that the vampires had been willing to burn down the shop where I'd worked and then track me to the library in order to get their hands on it. Now that Mortimer Vale was in jail, I could read the journal without the fear that a vampire would snatch the knowledge from my mind and use it against me... in theory, anyway. Evangeline, leader of the local vampires, had made no secret of her own desires to possess the knowledge the journal allegedly contained, and now she had my best friend Laney as potential leverage.

Not that Laney was afraid of her, though she probably should have been. My best friend was adjusting to her newly undead status better than I'd expected and had managed to wriggle out of staying with the other vampires in their ancient church, instead agreeing to take evening classes with the newbie vamps and live at the library the rest of the time. Since she slept during the day, I didn't worry that she might pick up on my thoughts as I read the journal.

I slid several sentences together and read the whole passage:

The book I am searching for supposedly belongs to a collector in rural Germany, but it's proving difficult to find the village where he lives. I believe it must be hidden under a magical shield of some kind, and without my wand, it's going to be difficult for me to find it. Though I had one stroke of good fortune: I am not the only person at the inn who is looking for that village. The inn's owner told me that a group of guests arrived the day before I did and were asking questions. He says they seem to sleep during the day and are prone to night-time wandering in the woods.

Why there are vampires at a location like this, I cannot say, though it is true that the dark forest is a natural habitat for them...

A shiver ran down my spine. He'd ended up staying at the same inn as a group of vampires. What were the odds that they'd been members of the Founders? Given the journal's apparent value to them, there was a fair chance, but he'd certainly been lucky to avoid them if he'd been staying at the same inn without a wand to defend himself with.

Part of me wondered if he'd known what he was getting himself into, but he'd been a young, newly married father of a toddler at the time. Risking his neck—in more than one way—wasn't a logical decision to make unless he'd had no choice in the matter, or he'd been unaware of the potential consequences of crossing that particular group of vamps. Considering the few mentions of the Founders I'd come across so far had been scribbled into the margins of the journal at a later date, I would guess the latter.

The library door opened, and a group of students entered. I laid down the journal to help them find the appropriate textbooks for their essays since Aunt Adelaide still hadn't returned from her trip to the hospital. Despite the interruption, I'd made some progress for once. I was starting to understand how my dad's hunt for ancient books had brought him on a collision course with the vampires, even if he hadn't known it at the time. He wouldn't have been able to resist the allure of a rare book. That much was consistent with my memories of him.

I spent the rest of the morning running around fetching books for the students, so the journal sat neglected on the desk until Aunt Adelaide returned around noon.

"Hey, Aunt Adelaide," I said. "Did they figure out the cause of death?"

"No, but they suspect the victim was cursed," she said. "Not my area of expertise, mind, but lethal curses are hard to pin down. Especially ones which leave no traces."

Strange. It wouldn't be the first time we'd run into an inexplicable death in town which left no apparent clues as to the cause, but the situation unnerved me all the same. "Do the police have any ideas about who might have been responsible?"

"I believe Edwin is questioning some individuals who were acquainted with the victim and saw him on the day of his death," she said. "The pool of suspects covers anyone the victim interacted with in recent days, but the curse might even have been cast from a distance, which complicates the matter."

"I bet." I hadn't studied curses in depth since they were one of the most complex types of magic, and my lessons hadn't progressed to that level, but unlike hexes or spells, they didn't necessarily have to be cast using a wand and weren't limited by location. For that reason, it was possible that the victim had been walking around with a curse on him for days or weeks without knowing until the instant he'd dropped dead. The only certainty was that a curse could have only been cast by a witch or wizard.

"I let them keep most of the books until they're done with them," Aunt Adelaide said. "It seemed the least I could do, but there's no doubt his death was murder."

"I imagine the Grim Reaper would have mentioned to the police if Rufus's ghost had said anything which pointed at who did it," I said. "I *think* he would. He was in an odd mood last night. In fact, he even told Xavier not to call the police."

"Why would he do that?"

"Presumably because it would fall under the category of 'interfering with human lives'." I gave an eye roll. "He needs to chill out, but I think he's regretting caving in and letting Xavier get a phone. Angels of Death don't send text messages, apparently."

His possessiveness was nothing new. Aunt Candace had posited the theory that the Grim Reaper was actually Xavier's biological father, but it didn't strike me as quite right given how the Grim Reaper seemed utterly ageless and inhuman. More likely was the fact that the Grim Reaper was starting to realise that Xavier and I weren't having a temporary fling but were committed to a long-term relationship, and he felt threatened as a result.

The truth of the matter was that I couldn't imagine *not* being with Xavier, an utterly new feeling to me which felt as dizzying as standing on the edge of a cliff—and trusting that if I fell, he'd catch me.

Aunt Adelaide's expression softened. "I'm sure Xavier is just as frustrated. He'll talk to the Grim Reaper, won't he?"

"He already has, but the guy is set in his ways," I said. "Occupational hazard of being a terrifying immortal that nobody dares stand up to."

"Give it time," she said. "He ought to see that Xavier is happier with you than he would be otherwise."

Honestly, right now, I'd take one date night with him which doesn't end in an unwanted interruption. Just one.

"I hope so." I stepped away from the desk. "Is it okay if I run over to Zee's and grab lunch? I can get you something too."

"Thanks for the offer, Rory," she said. "I know you've been watching the desk all morning. I'll take over for a while."

"Cheers." I retrieved my bag and then left the library, crossing the square towards the heavenly scent of baked goods.

Zee's usual smile was absent as I entered the bakery, her dark skin dusted with flour and her expression slightly downcast. She packed the muffins and cakes I'd ordered into a bag while I requested some extras to keep Estelle fortified.

"I bet she needs it," said Zee. "I wasn't very studious myself. I can't imagine staying at school into adulthood."

"Estelle is dedicated," I acknowledged. "Honestly, your cooking is divine enough that we'd all be missing out if you were writing essays instead."

She smiled. "Thanks. I was feeling pretty down this morning. Someone died out in the square last night. Can you believe it?"

"Oh," I said. "I saw... well, I was out with Xavier at the time, and we were on our way back to the library when they found him."

Her eyes rounded. "Oh, I forgot you were dating the Reaper. That must be weird. I mean, he's super hot, but he's also… I mean, if you run into dead bodies all the time, that's got to be a downer."

"We don't," I said. "Most of the time, anyway." Okay, my matter-of-fact tone probably didn't make me sound convincing.

Zee passed me the bag of goodies. "Rather you than me. Not that Xavier isn't stunning, but I prefer guys with beating hearts…"

She trailed off, her hands frozen on the bag while I turned towards the door to see none other than Xavier himself standing in the doorway.

"Oh." Clumsily, I rescued the bag from Zee before it slid from her hands. "Hey, Xavier. Did you want to buy something?"

He shook his head. "Can we talk outside for a second?"

My heart began to beat faster. "Sure. Hang on. I'll just pay."

I handed the cash over to a bemused Zee and left the bakery, my heart racing. *Can we talk* rarely led to anything good. Had the Grim Reaper finally pushed him into ending our relationship?

I gripped the paper bag in my hand and took the plunge. "What is it, Xavier?"

"The Grim Reaper," he said. "He's missing."

3

"What?" I dropped the bag, which luckily landed the right way up. "How can the *Grim Reaper* be missing?"

"He went out early this morning and never came back," Xavier said. "He often leaves the house without telling me where he's going, but I can generally sense his location. Not this time."

"You know he can be unpredictable." If Xavier was concerned for him, though, the Grim Reaper had gone a step too far.

"I might be overreacting, but he's never vanished off the radar before." His mouth pulled in a worried frown. "Not as far as I'm aware."

"You want to go and look for him, then?" Where would we even start? The guy could walk through walls and reach any location in minutes. We might as well try to track a kelpie from a boat.

"I've searched his usual haunts." He turned towards the

alleyway where we'd run into him last night. "He's not hanging around here, either, though I did wonder."

"Why, you don't think he might have been after the murderer from last night?" Hardly likely given his indifference to any human matters, murder included. "My aunt says the hospital staff have guessed a curse killed him. She loaned them some of the library's books to find out what it might have been."

"Really?" he said. "Strange."

"Yeah." I turned my back on the alleyway, shivering as a cold breeze swept across the square. "I promised my aunt I'd pick up lunch for her and Estelle, so I should go and drop this off. Then I can help you search for him if you like."

"You don't have to," he said. "Besides, I'd like to hear what your aunt has to say on the wizard's death."

"Okay." I crossed the square at his side, glad to have the chance to spend time with him despite the less-than-fortunate circumstances. *Missing?* The Grim Reaper didn't just disappear. Unless my annoyance over him interrupting our date had had unintended consequences, but I was pretty sure even the library's magic couldn't cause someone to disappear, let alone the Grim Reaper.

I re-entered the library and dropped off the bag of goodies on the desk, snagging a blueberry muffin for myself. "Aunt Adelaide, did any of the hospital staff mention seeing the Grim Reaper?"

She extracted a sandwich from the bag. "Definitely not. I think they'd have noticed him."

"Unless he was hiding in the shadows." I beckoned Xavier over to the desk. "Xavier didn't see the Grim Reaper escort the victim's soul to the afterlife, and he didn't get the chance to speak to his ghost, but he was curious about the lack of any obvious cause of death."

"Didn't your boss have anything to share with you?" Aunt Adelaide asked him.

"He doesn't usually give me any more than the barest details on the souls he escorts into the afterlife," said Xavier, keeping his answer vague. I didn't blame him for not wanting everyone to know that his boss was seemingly missing. "Rory said the people who examined his body thought it was a curse. Is that true?"

"I can't think of anything but a curse which might have caused a man to drop dead without leaving a mark on him," said Aunt Adelaide. "I gave them all the useful books I had on hand... except for the ones which require special permission to remove from the library, of course."

I frowned. "Special permission?"

"Means they're too advanced for you," Sylvester said from his perch on a nearby shelf. "Don't get any ideas."

"You don't need to tell me not to pick up dangerous books on curses," I said. "I take it those are the sort which are too dangerous to loan out to the general public?"

"Yes, that's right." Aunt Adelaide gave the owl a disapproving look. "I won't be consulting any of *those* titles unless absolutely necessary, though the library does contain the most extensive selection of books on curses in the region, much to a certain curse-breaker's annoyance."

I'd frankly forgotten the misanthropic local curse-breaker. Did *he* know an unknown curse had caused someone to drop dead?

"I guess the person who did it might have borrowed a book from here," I said. "Wouldn't be the first time."

"No, it wouldn't, unfortunately," said Aunt Adelaide.

"That said, none of our titles on offer to the public give information on how to *use* a curse to harm someone. Those books certainly exist, but they're heavily restricted and for good reason."

No kidding. The laws on curses were strict, and my family were only allowed to look after certain books on the condition that they kept them away from the public.

I finished my muffin and tossed the wrapper into the bin before calling Jet, my crow familiar. "Can you drop off some of these muffins outside Estelle's room?"

The little bird flew over and picked up the paper bag in his beak. "Yes, partner!"

Sylvester tried to steal a muffin as Jet flew past, but I gave him a stern look, and he left it alone. Meanwhile, I turned back to Xavier. "Want to head outside?"

If we hinted at the Grim Reaper's disappearance in front of Sylvester, he'd spread word to my entire family within the hour and probably half the public too. Xavier nodded. "Sure."

"Go ahead," said Aunt Adelaide. "Just remember to keep an eye on the time."

"Will do."

Xavier and I headed out of the library into the crisp, cold air. "I did say you didn't have to help me search, didn't I?"

"I know you didn't want to talk about you-know-what in front of a certain owl." My gaze landed on the alleyway where the body had been found. "Would there be any traces of the curse that killed the wizard over there?"

"If there were, I'd have seen them," he said. "There's a number of curses which leave no mark on their target. That's why it's so hard to find the caster a lot of the time."

"Do you think the curse-breaker knows?" I asked. "I mean, it's a bit late for him to break the curse if the victim is already dead, but I think the staff at the hospital might appreciate the help."

"Would *you* want the curse-breaker hanging around while you try to solve a murder?" he said. "Honestly, if he's as rude to you as he was before, I'm not going to stand for it."

"Last time we spoke, he actually apologised for some of his earlier rudeness," I said. "But you're right... visiting him isn't exactly my idea of a good time."

The curse-breaker and my grandmother hadn't been friendly since he'd had a close-up experience with the library's magic when my family had hired him to try to untangle the spells on the library when they'd inherited it from Grandma after her death. While they'd been glad of his failure to penetrate its web of secrets, he saw us as bad news, and the feeling was more or less mutual.

Xavier and I walked past the clock tower to the seafront and made for the shop where the curse-breaker spent his time. Mr Bennet, tall and thin with a sour face which rarely brightened with a smile, did not look thrilled when the pair of us entered the bare, dimly lit room which comprised his shop.

"You," he said—not directed at me but at Xavier. "I already told your boss I can't help him."

"The Grim Reaper?" Xavier said. "He was here? Today?"

"I assumed he told you."

Huh? Why had the Grim Reaper paid a visit to the curse-breaker? And why had he then given his apprentice the slip?

"He didn't," said Xavier. "Might I ask what you discussed with one another?"

Mr Bennet's expression shuttered. "If he didn't tell you, it's not my place to spread the details, especially in front of human witnesses."

"If it's about that guy who died from a curse, that's why we're here too," I said to him. "We want to know—"

"I'm a curse-breaker, not a homicide detective," he growled. "The police have already been pestering me. I can't locate a curse out of nothing at all."

"There really are no clues?" I asked. "Surely you at least know which types of curse can cause someone to drop dead."

"Do you know how many types of illegal curses there are?"

"A hundred and twelve." I'd memorised that fact early on, partly due to Aunt Candace's tendency to go off on tangents during our magic lessons. "There's got to be a way to narrow it down, and you're the expert, not me."

My feeble attempt to placate him went nowhere. "I can *break* curses. Anything else is out of my area of expertise."

"Then why did the Grim Reaper visit you?" I glanced at Xavier. "If not to ask about the murder?"

"Ask him yourself."

Honestly. The guy was as stubborn as a manticore. Frustratingly, Xavier *might* have been able to ask his boss… if not for his inconvenient absence.

"He doesn't like me," I settled for saying. "He also sees himself as an impartial entity who doesn't intervene in human affairs, so he won't share evidence with the police."

"Am I supposed to care?"

"When someone was murdered?" I raised a brow. "Yes, absolutely. Besides, you aren't bound by Reaper laws. Have you had any odd requests for help with curses lately which might have struck you as suspicious? Questions on illegal curses?"

"No," he said. "Certainly not the sort of curses which would end in someone dead. The only strange person I've seen in the last week was from out of town, and he wanted to ask for advice on renting a property on the seafront, not curses."

"Who was that?"

"Irrelevant." He indicated the door. "Now kindly leave me in peace."

Sensing we'd face a losing battle if we stayed, Xavier and I left the curse-breaker's shop and walked out onto the seafront.

"Maybe I should have told him my boss is missing," Xavier said. "I didn't think that would make him any more likely to share what he knows, but until he comes back, I have nobody else to question. Why he'd opt to visit the curse-breaker is a mystery to me."

"You and me both." I shivered in the cold air. "I can think of a way to bring him back, though. The Grim Reaper, I mean."

He arched a brow. "Like what?"

"Arrange a date," I said. "Put as much planning into it as possible, and I can guarantee he'll find a way to show up and ruin it."

Xavier's mouth quirked, then the amusement bled from his expression. "That doesn't say much for our dating life or for my efforts to make this as normal a relationship as possible."

"It's hardly your fault," I said. "Besides, my family has caused easily as much trouble as yours has. Not that the Grim Reaper really counts as family…"

Or did he? I wasn't sure. Xavier had never told me about his birth family, but Reapers weren't supposed to acknowledge their former lives. He'd made a lot of allowances for me already, considering Reapers also weren't allowed to *have* relationships with regular people. That alone proved he was willing to get around the restrictions usually imposed on him.

The slight problem? If the Grim Reaper had disappeared for good, then Xavier would have to take over as Reaper full-time.

"Tonight, then," he said. "We'll go to the Black Dog again. Or is there somewhere else you'd prefer?"

Somewhere without any annoying giggling onlookers if such a place was possible… but there wasn't anywhere that Xavier wouldn't draw attention. Being the Reaper's apprentice made the stares inevitable.

"No, that's fine," I said. "Ah—wait, the poetry night is on at the library. I'm supposed to help out with that."

A thoughtful expression passed over his face. "I'm not supposed to show up to frivolous human events which aren't appropriate to my position of impartiality, so that might work instead."

"It's a poetry night, not an orgy."

Xavier choked on a surprised laugh. "Honestly, the latter would probably be less offensive to him."

"So that's where we've been going wrong?"

A smile tugged at his mouth. "It's not really my scene. I'm more into one person at a time. Or one in particular, anyway."

Warmth pooled inside me as he caught my hand and pulled me into a kiss. Despite the delicious heat of his touch, the back of my mind ticked over the implication that he wanted to be intimate with me. We'd never discussed the subject in depth, mostly because being alone in a room with him was almost impossible. The library was teeming with potential interruptions, and *his* home contained the Grim Reaper. Or it usually did, anyway.

He broke off the kiss and smiled. "See you tonight, then?"

"We'll see if your grumpy boss shows his face at the poetry night," I said. "Might be memorable, if nothing else." Or horrifying.

"I'll walk you back to the library."

He did so while I wished we could have had more time together, especially with his boss out of the picture for the time being. It struck me that we might be letting an opportunity go to waste, but with Estelle busy and Aunt Adelaide liable to end up being called back to the hospital at any moment, that left me as the only person who could watch the front desk at the library. Aunt Candace had been relegated to the back room after the incident with the kids and the vampire's basement, while Cass had got herself temporarily banned from the front desk for teaming up with Sylvester and making several students cry over late fees.

Naturally, as soon as I entered the library, Aunt Adelaide beckoned me to the desk. "Good timing. I've been called back to the hospital to bring some more books."

My heart dropped. "Did they find anything more about the curse?"

"They said they'd give me the details in person," she said. "I'll give you an update when I'm back."

"Sure," I replied. "Ah—is it okay if Xavier comes to the poetry night?"

"Of course," she said. "Why wouldn't it be?"

"Just checking."

In the meantime, I pondered on how else we might take advantage of our temporary Grim Reaper-free status. I'd debated inviting him to stay over at the library, but Sylvester's habit of flying into my room and my aunt's nosy tendencies made me reluctant to accidentally cause a repeat of the incident when I'd invited him to dinner with my family and they'd launched an interrogation.

When the alternative was a sleepover in the graveyard, it might be worth the risk, but my control over the library's magic was slippery at best. The chances of us getting a moment of privacy were lower than the odds of the vampire in his basement getting up and walking around.

Suppressing a sigh, I made a mental note to ask Estelle about privacy spells—assuming her thesis didn't eat her alive in the meantime, that is.

4

Aunt Adelaide stayed out for the rest of the afternoon, leaving me in charge of the front desk. I also ended up handling most of the book requests too. While it was gratifying to know that my aunt trusted me to handle this level of responsibility, I wished one of the others would lend a hand. Meaning Aunt Candace or Cass, because Estelle at least had good reason to be shut in her room. It seemed the rest of my dad's journal would have to wait until later.

Estelle didn't reappear until the early evening, when she finally shuffled into the lobby, looking rather like Aunt Candace while she was on a deadline, her hair like a bird's nest and yet more books in her arms. "Hey, Rory. My mum didn't leave you in charge all day, did she?"

"She didn't have much choice," I said. "She's been at the hospital all day, helping them figure out what curse was used on that wizard who died."

"Someone died?"

"Where have you been?" Sylvester said.

"You know where she's been," I pointed out. "Sorry, Estelle. A wizard was found dead last night, and he seems to have died from a curse which didn't leave a mark on him."

Estelle's eyes widened. "Whoa. I definitely didn't hear *that.* Why'd they ask my mum to help?"

"They borrowed all our books on curses—except the high-security ones, that is," I said. "I think they wanted her to help narrow down what kind of curse it was."

"They must be short on ideas, then," she said. "Mum isn't an expert on curses. That'd be Mr Bennet, though I bet he wasn't falling over himself to help out."

"Got it in one," I said. "Xavier and I paid him a visit, but he said that he didn't know anything about the curse and pretty much threw us out."

"Sounds like him." Her jaw cracked when she yawned. "I wish I could help, but I haven't even been outside in days."

"That can't be good," I said. "You don't have to turn into a complete recluse, you know."

"I know, but I want this essay to be done," she said. "If I really buckle down, I can get it done by the end of the week and then get back to business as usual."

"Okay, if you're sure," I said. "Have you ever heard of a curse causing someone to drop dead without leaving a mark on them before?"

"No." She yawned again. "I'm guessing it's under the top rank of illegal spells and worthy of a life sentence in prison if they get caught. I've been up to my neck in textbooks on magical law lately, so I should know."

"Someone must have really had a grudge against that wizard, then."

The tricky part about curses was that the caster could put conditions on them which would make it hard for anyone to trace who'd actually used the curse. If the curse was placed on an object, for instance, the caster wouldn't need to have any contact with the target at all, while the curse could be set to activate after a certain length of time or in a certain place. In other words, the easiest way to find the perpetrator was to start with people the victim had known and who might have had any possible reason to slam him with a lethal curse.

Estelle approached the desk. "I can take over here for a bit if you want to indulge your curiosity about curses."

"Nah, there's nowhere for me to read up on the basics with most of the books gone," I said. "Except the Book of Questions, and I'm not sure even that can help in this scenario."

The Book could theoretically answer one question from each of us per day but also had an annoying tendency to avoid giving anyone a straight answer regardless of the vast stores of knowledge it contained. If information on the right curse existed inside one of the high-security books, the Book of Questions might be able to point me in the right direction, but the books which lay behind locked doors tended to have nasty side effects on people who picked them up without permission. Since none other than Sylvester controlled the Forbidden Room which lay inside the Book, he'd be highly amused if I landed myself in a trap.

No, if they'd been barred from public access, it was for good reason. Besides, it was getting increasingly hard to reference the Book of Questions without giving away that I knew Sylvester was the actual repository of the knowledge of the entire library. Nobody else in the family knew, since I'd guessed by complete accident.

"Nah, the Book of Questions isn't really made for catching killers." Estelle scanned the desk, and her gaze landed on the translator document. "You've been working on the journal?"

"Yeah," I said. "I actually got to read it for more than five minutes earlier, which is an improvement on my dating life."

Estelle winced. "I hope that *isn't* accurate, Rory, but that's annoying on both counts. Did you find out anything interesting from the journal?"

"My dad went on a trip to Europe to find rare books from a magically hidden location in rural Germany when I was a toddler," I said. "It sounds like he ran into some vampires in the same place, and I wondered if that might be where it started. Their enmity, I mean."

Her mouth formed an 'O' of understanding. "You think he ran afoul of the vampires because they were after the same rare book as he was?"

"Possibly," I said. "The vamps had the advantage, though. He was playing human at the time and didn't even have his wand. I haven't found out how it turned out yet since I've been run off my feet ever since I got back from visiting the curse-breaker."

"You said you visited Mr Bennet with Xavier, right?" she said. "So you did get to spend a little time together, at least. I never asked how your date last night went, did I?"

"It went fine until the Grim Reaper called Xavier to his side," I said. "Except he'd already escorted the soul of the dead wizard to the afterlife himself. He just wanted to drag Xavier away from me."

"Okay, *that* is uncalled for," she said. "Did Xavier stand up to him?"

"We both tried, but it's like trying to argue with a kelpie," I said. "As for our visit to the curse-breaker, that was a dead end."

"Did you ask Mr Bennet if he knew of anyone experimenting with illegal curses, then?"

"He claimed nobody has asked him any dodgy questions," I said. "Except the Grim Reaper allegedly paid him a visit at some point last night, after the murder, and neither of them would tell us why."

"Whoa." Her lips pursed. "I guess the Grim Reaper was the one who discovered the body, but maybe he *did* know it was a curse that killed him. Did Mr Bennet give anything else away?"

"All he said was that someone was asking questions about buying property on the seafront," I said. "But that has nothing to do with curses. He was just trying to get rid of us."

"I bet." She glanced up at the clock. "Almost closing time. We'd better start getting the Reading Corner set up for the poetry night as soon as everyone clears off."

As the last patrons were leaving the library, Laney peered out of the corridor to my family's living quarters. My best friend looked almost the same as her human self, albeit a glossier and more graceful version even dressed in jogging trousers and a hoodie with her dark-brown hair pulled into a messy bun.

"Hey." I walked over to her. "Are you coming to the poetry night?"

"I have a lesson this evening." She pulled a face. "With the baby vampires. In fairness, some of the newbies are older than I am, but some aren't. Vampire kids are creepy."

"Being a vampire child can't be fun for them either." Vampires wound up stuck in time the instant they turned, eternally frozen at the age they'd been when they'd died. "Look on the bright side. At least you're not stuck as a pimply teenager forever."

"Ha," she said. "No sparkles here either. Not that I've seen anyway. But you're right. At least I don't have to get asked for ID for the rest of my eternal life."

I gave her a smile. "Yeah, that would suck."

"Rory, that was terrible." She snorted.

"Hey, Xavier thinks I'm amusing."

"Are you seeing him tonight?"

"He said he *might* come to the poetry night, but it's not really his scene."

"Can't imagine it is," she said. "You did at least get a date yesterday, right?"

"Before the Grim Reaper interrupted." I stopped myself before I started recounting the whole experience, since if she saw Evangeline tonight, the head vampire would likely pluck every piece of information I shared with her from her mind.

"Oh." She looked away. "Sorry. Why is it that every time you start thinking about not wanting me to read your thoughts, my mind starts drifting in that direction?"

"It's not really your fault, though," I reassured her. "It's a reflex, isn't it?"

"Yeah." She gave a sheepish look. "I'm getting more control over it with every lesson. It's just tricky. Like trying not to float when there's no gravity."

"That's good news, then," I said. "If you manage to get

some control over your mind-reading, you'll also be able to prevent other vampires doing the same to you."

"Yeah, I can't wait to be able to lock Evangeline out of my thoughts."

I wasn't sure if she'd ever be able to permanently stop the head vampire from nosing into her mind, considering the ability tended to be hierarchical, with the strongest vampires able to bar the weakest from reading their thoughts but not vice versa. Evangeline, whose mind was closed even to the strongest vampires, sat right at the top of the food chain, and few could best her. Regardless, Laney was stubborn enough to give it a fair shot, I was sure.

"Good luck," I said. "Unless you want to stay for dinner?"

"Nah, human food doesn't really appeal anymore."

"Guess not." Nowadays, Laney mostly lived on supplies sourced from the local blood bank at the hospital. Which was better than the alternative if nothing else. "See you later."

She waved me off while I headed back to the Reading Corner to help Estelle get the library ready for the poetry night and tried not to think about Evangeline playing mind games with my best friend.

The only upside of my close proximity to the Grim Reaper was that it was a useful way to keep Evangeline at arm's length—in theory, anyway. The Reapers and the vampires were traditionally enemies, maybe because vampires skirted around surrendering to a natural death and instead lived forever, while Reapers' jobs were to evict the souls of the dead from this realm. Evangeline's attempts to gain the trust of my best friend remained a thorn in my side despite Laney's determination to resist her. I sincerely hoped I'd refrained from accidentally letting any thoughts slip through concerning the Grim Reaper's unwelcome absence, because that would be of entirely too much interest to the scheming vampire leader.

Since Aunt Adelaide remained absent, Estelle and I made dinner—or rather, Estelle did most of the work, probably out of guilt over being shut in her room all day. I wasn't much of a cook, so I was glad for her help. Aunt Adelaide finally showed up shortly after we'd doled out helpings of bangers and mash on plates, and Aunt Candace and Cass made a reappearance for the first time all day. If you asked me, they'd both been trying to avoid picking up any extra responsibilities in the library while Aunt Adelaide was out.

"There you are," I said. "Are either of you two going to help out with the poetry night?"

"No, I'm on a deadline," Aunt Candace replied.

"You weren't this morning." Aunt Adelaide sat down next to her at the table.

"I am now," said Aunt Candace, digging into her mashed potatoes. "Besides, listening to other people read their poetry makes me break out in hives."

"I doubt that's true." I glanced at Estelle, who was nodding off in her seat. "Come on, Estelle deserves the night off, and I can't wrangle a dozen or more amateur poets single-handedly."

"I'll help," said Aunt Adelaide. "It's no bother."

Estelle blinked awake. "No, I'll do it. The poetry night was my idea, after all."

Cass made a sceptical noise. "Your wannabe poets might take offence if you fall asleep."

"Better than when you gave them feedback on the go and made them cry," said Estelle.

Cass scowled. "They're mostly *terrible* poets, though. I did the English language a favour by stopping them."

"You aren't going to be called back to the hospital?" I asked Aunt Adelaide, more to distract the others from their argument than anything else. "Have they found out what type of curse was responsible for Rufus's death?"

"No," Aunt Adelaide said. "However, it's not really an appropriate topic for the dinner table."

"Oh, come on. He only dropped dead," said Aunt Candace. "It's not as though his skin fell off or he exploded."

"That's quite enough of that, Candace," said Aunt Adelaide. "The truth is that they still aren't sure, but there are reasons for concern, and we'll talk about them later."

And that was that. We finished our meals, after which Aunt Candace and Cass vanished to their rooms. Aunt Adelaide cleared away the dishes while Estelle went to make some more last-minute preparations for the poetry night. I, meanwhile, waited for Xavier, crossing my fingers behind my back that the Grim Reaper didn't pick tonight to make his sudden return to town. Maybe I shouldn't have tried tempting fate by inviting his apprentice to a poetry night of all things, but when Xavier showed up, it was without any sign of his shadowy boss. That alone made it worth the risk, and so did the kiss he gave me on the doorstep.

"Glad you could make it," I said. "No sign of you-know-who?"

"None," he murmured. "Makes me wish we could take the night off."

My heart skipped a beat. "Me, too, but Estelle's practically dead on her feet, and Aunt Adelaide isn't much better, considering she was rushing around at the hospital all day. Someone has to help wrangle the aspiring poets."

He raised a brow. "What, do you think they'd start a riot without anyone to keep an eye on them?"

"Don't speak too soon."

The sound of loud conversation drifted over as a group of witches and wizards I'd never seen before approached the library, congregating around a wizard with bright-pink hair that stuck up as though he'd trodden on an open plug socket. The new arrival swaggered into the library without so much as taking note of me and Xavier, his entourage tailing after him.

"Who was that?" I whispered.

"No clue," Xavier muttered back. "He must be new in town."

I was fairly sure I'd have recalled seeing a newcomer with hair bright enough to be a traffic hazard, but I guessed the poetry night had attracted some new members. At the very least, Estelle would be relieved to know that neglecting her role in charge of social events while she worked on her thesis hadn't hurt the popularity of the weekly poetry night.

Xavier and I headed into the library, where softly glowing lanterns hovered above the shelves and cast an aura of cosiness around the Reading Corner. The various beanbags, chairs, and hammocks had been rearranged into a circle with space for each poet to stand in the centre when their turn came to read aloud. Estelle and

Aunt Adelaide supervised from the sidelines as the rest of the aspiring poets filed into the library. Both of them appeared mildly startled at the sight of the pink-haired newcomer, who'd sprawled across a beanbag. His companions occupied the seats around him, chatting loudly and paying zero attention to the rest of us.

When the seats were mostly full, Estelle clapped her hands to call for silence. "Welcome to the poetry night, everyone. For those of you who are new here, we'll typically take it in turns to read one poem each, and if there's spare time at the end, then you can have another turn. Does that sound reasonable?"

"Sure," said the pink-haired guy. "Should I go first?"

"Yes!" chorused his followers, to the general bemusement of everyone else in the room.

Was he some kind of celebrity? His followers were certainly acting like it, and they even broke into applause when he swaggered over to the circle's centre.

"I'm Nero the Wonder," he announced. "I'm visiting your beautiful little town to scout out locations for my own studio."

"Have you heard of him?" I whispered to Xavier, who shook his head.

Estelle, however, leaned over from the chair on my other side. "He's famous on the Wizarding Web. I thought I recognised him from somewhere."

"Famous for doing what?"

Nero the Wonder waved his wand and conjured up a flurry of butterflies, which flew into the air to a chorus of gasps from the crowd. Apparently, this was a known routine, because his followers were soon clamouring for more conjuring tricks and flinging praise at him.

Estelle cleared her throat. "Apologies for interrupting, but this is a poetry night, and we have a lot of people waiting for their turn. Can you please read your poem?"

"Calm down, sweetheart," he said. "This is all part of the show. You get me?"

"Yeah, it's part of the show," drawled a wizard who appeared to be wearing a T-shirt with Nero the Wonder's face imprinted on it. *Good lord.*

"You have ten minutes maximum." Estelle's words were drowned out with boos from his followers, and she fell silent with an uncharacteristic scowl on her face. When she tried to speak again, the crowd's gasps of awe interrupted when Nero the Wonder conjured up a giant dragon that swooped around the balconies above our heads. As it breathed a streak of illusory fire, he began to speak.

"I am Nero the Wonder," he said. "When it rains, I can make it thunder…"

More terrible rhyming followed while I found myself wishing he'd just stuck with the conjuring instead. After ten minutes of drivel, he finished by making the dragon vanish in a puff of smoke, which left his admirers gasping in awe. Two of them were crying openly, while another had conjured a banner shaped like Nero the Wonder's head and was loudly calling for an encore.

"That's enough," said Estelle. "That was certainly a memorable performance. If we have time at the end, then you're welcome to read another poem…"

Please no. I'd almost rather the Grim Reaper *had* interrupted.

Nero the Wonder gave the crowd a cheery wave. "That's it for the night. Thank you for being here, and don't forget to check out my channel on the Wizarding Web."

He flicked his wand, and an explosion of confetti rained over our heads, spelling out his name and his website details in the middle of the circle. While we were all picking bits of confetti out of our hair, he headed for the library's exit with his entourage following him like a swarm of ducklings.

"He can't be the guy Mr Bennet was talking about?" I whispered to Xavier. "You know, who was asking about prices for real estate on the coast?"

Xavier removed a handful of pink confetti from his blond curls. "If he is, I hope he picks somewhere else to set up his studio."

That I could agree on. "I somehow doubt he put a fatal curse on someone. Doesn't seem showy enough for him."

Though by his fan club's behaviour, they might well have been willing to curse anyone who insulted Nero the Wonder. When one of the other attenders of the poetry night protested at them leaving early, no fewer than five members of the entourage returned to heckle him.

"Nero is very busy," said a girl with her hair dyed the same pink shade as her idol. "He has a lot of important stuff to do. You get me?"

"That's quite enough," Estelle said. "If you're leaving, then please close the door behind you."

Everyone breathed a collective sigh of relief when the last member of his fan club had disappeared, at which point Estelle cast an instant vanishing charm to get rid of the rest of the confetti.

"Sorry you had to sit through that performance," I said

to Xavier. "I wouldn't have blamed you for using your shadow trick to sneak out."

He chuckled. "I have to admit, I was tempted to for a moment back then."

I took back my brief thoughts on his boss potentially rescuing us from Nero's poetry, since throwing pink confetti at the Grim Reaper was definitely worthy of finding oneself on the receiving end of his scythe.

In the meantime, Xavier and I returned our attention to the next poet, who was thankfully more bearable than Nero the Wonder's performance. I could only assume his conjuring tricks had won him his fame, because it definitely wasn't his poetry skills. Even after Estelle's quick actions, we kept finding bits of confetti everywhere, and all of them seemed to have Nero the Wonder's website details on them.

"He's a creative marketer, I'll say that much." I crumpled another piece of confetti in my hand and tossed it in the bin as we watched the other attendees leave the library at the end of the evening. "We could learn a few tricks from him."

"Do you need to advertise the library by throwing around confetti with your address printed on it?" Xavier asked.

"Probably not," I relented. "Also, our magic doesn't work as well outside of the library, so fancy conjuring tricks might be out of reach if we want to advertise on the other side of the country."

Not that we needed to do any more advertising. The library was as popular as ever, as was the poetry night, and once Estelle had handed her thesis in, she'd be able to return to her full-time position as head of social events.

As for me? I turned to Xavier as the last of the poets left the library. "He really didn't show up. Your boss, I mean."

"I know." His voice was low, with a hint of concern. "I've searched the entire town at least twice."

"And there's nowhere else he might be?"

"There are a few places," he said, "but the problem is that I can't pinpoint his general direction, let alone anything else."

"What, like a compass pointing you towards him?"

"More or less," he said. "We're bound as master and apprentice, which means that theoretically, I can step into the shadows and transport myself to his side without conscious effort. Even *that* isn't working."

"Whoa." That sounded like serious cause for concern, but if Xavier couldn't find his boss, the rest of us had no chance. Unless the library contained a hitherto-unknown section on finding missing Reapers.

Hmm. The Book of Questions *might* be able to give me an idea, but asking the book would involve exposing the Grim Reaper's absence to Sylvester, who'd spread it around the whole library by the morning. Especially if Laney accidentally read my thoughts and news reached the hands of the head vampire. I could only imagine how Evangeline might take advantage of her most powerful adversary's absence.

Xavier drew me into a hug. "I don't want to worry you, Rory. I'm sure there's an explanation I haven't thought of yet."

"I wish I could help." Who—or what—could possibly send the Grim Reaper packing? Or had he left of his own accord and neglected to tell his apprentice? That was the best-case scenario, though it didn't paint him in a particularly good light. "You don't think he went away on purpose, do you?"

"It would be a great relief to me if that turned out to be true," he said. "Considering the alternatives."

I shivered, leaning into Xavier's warmth. "Yeah, no kidding."

"The other possibility is that he got called away on an urgent mission," said Xavier. "Which means he ought to return soon. Most Reaper missions don't take long."

"If he's got himself into trouble, would rescuing him be enough for him to be grateful towards me?" I said half-jokingly. "Enough for him to give us some peace for once?"

"Don't count on it."

I gave an eye roll. "Worth a try."

If someone could overpower the Grim Reaper, though, I doubted *I'd* fare any better against them. Yet I wanted to help, if just for Xavier's peace of mind. I'd never seen him this rattled before.

"Rory?" Estelle called from the Reading Corner. "Can you give me a hand over here? Nero the Wonder's entourage left a huge mess to clean up, and there's confetti *inside* the beanbags."

Typical. "I'll be over in a second."

Xavier took a step back. "I'll drop by tomorrow, and we can go for a proper date. That okay?"

I pressed my lips to his. "Sure."

5

The following morning started with a magic lesson with Aunt Candace, who was as inconsistent a teacher as she was at everything else. Generally, her lessons considered of her throwing random lectures at me about whatever subject was the focus of her attention lately. Once she'd had enough coffee, anyway.

After draining her second coffee cup, she said, "You've already covered most of the Grade Two textbook, so we're going to move to Grade Three today."

I shifted in my seat. "Just so you know, if we're starting with the first chapter, I already read it."

"Well, aren't *you* an overachiever." She tutted at me. "And the second chapter?"

"That too." Reading chapters of my textbooks was generally an easier task to fit into spare minutes than the more labour-intensive work of translating my dad's journal. "I haven't got to the part about familiar training yet, though."

"I thought that familiar of yours was acting as Estelle's packhorse," she said. "Honestly. *She's* an overachiever too. I never saw much point in traditional forms of education. What's a PhD in magical history and law going to do for you?"

"Help you win arguments?" I suggested.

Aunt Candace snorted. "I expect you'll go down the same path as Estelle when you catch her up. Really, most of these Grade Three spells aren't much good for practical use."

"Is there a locking spell in there somewhere?" I asked.

"You can use a locking spell with your biblio-witch magic, can't you?" True. Since I was also learning biblio-witch magic on more of a need-to-know basis, I already knew some effective substitutes for using a wand.

"Yes, but they aren't always as effective outside of the library." In response to her sceptical look, I added, "Anyway, it'd be handy to have an alternative which is more... owl-proof. How do you stop Sylvester from disturbing you when you're writing?"

"Oh, he knows not to bother me when I'm working," she said. "Why would you want to lock Sylvester out of your room?"

"You know he keeps waking me up at the crack of dawn." I let the subject drop before she guessed the real reason. "Never mind. Is there anything on curses in the Grade Three textbook?"

A grin came to her mouth. "You're curious about the poor wizard who dropped dead the other night, are you?"

"It's hard not to be," I said. "Considering Aunt Adelaide spend most of yesterday at the hospital helping the staff figure out the cause of death, but she was cagey about answering any of our questions yesterday."

She gave me a considering look. "If you ask me, she suspects the killer got the information on how to use the curse from the library. That's why she's reluctant to share any details."

"That can't be it," I said. "People have used the library's resources to learn how to commit crimes before, and she's never hidden anything from us."

"Curses are among the worst things you can use magic for," she said. "This one is particularly perplexing because there's no obvious suspect. This Rufus person was a wizard who worked at the local bank who didn't have any enemies. Not much to work with there."

Hmm. Doubtless Edwin would not be thrilled if I showed up at the police station and started asking him questions, because despite my family's access to the books about curses, we weren't directly involved in the investigation. I might have found it easier to put the issue out of mind if the Grim Reaper hadn't disappeared shortly after finding the wizard's body... and after visiting the curse-breaker's shop.

"Even if he didn't have any obvious enemies, someone seemingly cursed him to death," I said. "I know there's a *lot* of illegal curses, but how many of them can cause someone to drop dead and not leave a mark on them?"

"More than you'd think," she said. "I've used at least three of them as murder weapons in my books, but I find them impersonal and unimaginative for the most part. Now, stop trying to distract me, and open your textbook before my sister comes to reprimand both of us."

And that was that. I opened the textbook and returned

to work. I'd barely scratched the surface on basic curses, so it'd be months or even years before I got to the advanced sort.

Once my lesson came to an end, I went to prepare for the library to open for the day. Aunt Adelaide sat behind the front desk, flipping through the record book with Sylvester watching over her. Unlike me, she didn't seem to mind the owl sitting at her shoulder while she worked.

Aunt Adelaide glanced up. "Hello, Rory."

"Hey," I said. "Are you going back to the hospital today?"

"Not unless they need me there," she said. "I might have to go and pick up the books they've finished with at some point, but that won't take too long."

"So they know what type of curse it was?" I asked.

She drew in a breath. "The curse was an experimental one. That is, a curse created by the user, or so it seems. It wasn't made with reference to any of our books, anyway."

I blinked. "Wait, how is that possible?"

"There are other books out there," she said. "Most are banned, of course, but a determined person can certainly find them if they're so inclined."

I found my thoughts drifting to my dad's long journey to get his hands on a rare book. A book the library didn't have, I assumed. There'd certainly be titles which were one of a kind, even in the magical world, but why on earth would someone here in Ivory Beach go looking for a book without using the library? And why would they go to such extreme lengths to commit murder when there were other, less time-intensive means of doing so?

Sylvester clucked his beak. "Yes, there are. And with

magic involved, anything is possible given enough persistence."

"It doesn't help that we have no idea how long he was actually cursed for," added Aunt Adelaide. "The curse stopped his heart and then caused him to drop dead without him even knowing he was cursed. At least, he didn't mention it to anyone."

"That's horrible," I said.

"That's dark magic for you," said Sylvester. "I find it unimaginative, personally."

"Aunt Candace said the same," I said. "Good way to avoid getting caught, though. Do *you* have any theories?"

"No," he said. "I prefer not to twist my brain in knots over such things. Neither should you if you know what's good for you."

Maybe, but the Grim Reaper vanished the same night he died. I can't overlook that link, especially with Xavier left in the dark as to where he disappeared to.

"Don't you think it's strange that someone without any enemies would be murdered in such a complicated way?" I asked. "I mean, it's not exactly straightforward, cursing someone. It takes a ton of preparation from what I've heard, and they'd have had to hide all the evidence."

"Have you been talking to Candace, by any chance?" Sylvester said. "I expect she's in her element, eagerly coming up with a dozen theories of her own, whatever she might say about the lack of imagination in the killer."

"Of course she is," said Aunt Adelaide, turning the page of the record book. "Ah, *there* it is. I was beginning to wonder who had that textbook."

"Which book?" I asked.

"A book on curses similar to the one which might have

been used on Rufus." She ran a finger down the page. "We loaned it out two weeks ago. That would explain why I couldn't find it."

I frowned. "Who has it?"

"A professor at the local university who took it out for research purposes," she said. "He was due to return it in a couple of days. I wonder if we might convince him to give it back a day early."

"I can ask," I offered.

"Are you sure, Rory?" Aunt Adelaide said. "I think Estelle is too busy to go with you. And Sylvester doesn't like the university campus."

The owl shuffled his wings. "Their library is pitiful for a so-called centre of knowledge."

"Everyone comes here anyway, as well you know." I hadn't been back to the campus for a while, but I remembered the way. "I'll take Jet with me. Who's the professor?"

"Professor Colt," she said. "I'll open the library and stay at the front while you're gone. Would you be able to bring the book straight here? I'd rather give it a check before I hand it over to the hospital staff."

"Of course."

It looked as though today would be another busy one, but as long as I had a date with Xavier later, I'd deal with whatever the universe saw fit to throw my way. I called Jet, my crow familiar, on my way to the door. I'd rather have his company than Sylvester's, so I didn't mind leaving the owl with Aunt Adelaide instead.

"I'm off to the university campus to fetch a book," I said to Jet. "Want to come with me?"

"Yes, partner!" He flew in excited circles around my head as I opened the library door.

There, I found Xavier waiting for me outside. "Hey, Rory."

"Hey," I said, surprised. "How did you know I was leaving?"

"Lucky guess," he said. "Did your aunt send you on an errand?"

"Yeah, I'm supposed to pick up a book from a professor at the university," I said. "Might be to do with the curse that killed the wizard. Have you seen—?"

"No, he's still not back," he said. "That's not why I came to see you, though. I hoped we might be able to make plans for later."

Jet interrupted by flying around my head again, cawing excitedly. "Sure, that'd be great. Want to come to campus with me? If today's as busy as I think it'll be, then this might be our only chance to talk until this evening."

He fell into step with me as I headed across the square. "Did you say the book you're after is connected to the curse which killed that wizard?"

"According to my Aunt Adelaide, it might contain some useful information on that type of curse," I said. "The professor is supposed to return it in a couple of days anyway, so I offered to ask if he'd be willing to give it back early. Since nobody knows who killed Rufus, all we can really do is look at the method of his death and work from there."

"Strange," he murmured. "As strange as the fact that the only witness is…"

"Not around," I finished vaguely in case anyone was listening in. Which they weren't, because the high street wasn't particularly busy at the moment. "Definitely suspicious timing, whether he's connected or not."

Jet flew overhead as we walked uphill and past the church where the local vampires made their home while Xavier's gaze drifted in that direction. "I hope a certain person hasn't heard about his absence."

"Same," I said. "I didn't tell my family, or Laney, either, and I don't *think* she picked it up from my thoughts. She's still hoping to be able to learn to block her thoughts from being read, but master vampires like you-know-who are leagues ahead of everyone else."

Xavier nodded. "I do wonder if she's seen him lately, but I won't give her the satisfaction of asking."

"Best not give her the ammunition to use against us." Of all the people in town who might stand to take advantage of the Grim Reaper's absence, Evangeline sat at the very top of the list. The scheming head vampire was manipulative on a good day, and she took great enjoyment in taunting me about my dad's journal. She'd only backed off on trying to trick me into letting her get her paws on it when Laney had been turned into a vampire, and that was because she hoped to read the information from her thoughts instead.

Xavier and I entered the university campus, which consisted of a collection of brick buildings of varying sizes and shapes in a haphazard arrangement. I had to ask for directions three times before a harried undergrad student pointed us towards a squarish building that looked as though it'd had its roof replaced at least once—which, given the side effects of magical experimentation, might well have been the case. Had the curse which had caused a wizard to drop dead originated here too?

After taking several wrong turnings, I found my way

to the right office, labelled Professor Colt, Theoretical Magic. "Want to wait outside?"

"Best if I do, I think," Xavier said. "I'll be out here if you need me, okay?"

"Sure," I said. "Keep an eye on Jet and make sure he doesn't fly into any of the offices."

From the series of loud bangs emanating from the floor above, someone was engaged in magical experimentation. Or perhaps trying to move a filing cabinet. Hoping the ceiling was sturdier than it looked, I knocked on the door.

"Come in!" said a hoarse voice.

I opened the door and walked into a small office filled with cabinets and bookshelves piled high with textbooks. No magical explosions that I could see. Instead, a man wearing a faded suit and tie poked his balding head out from behind a cabinet. "And you are...?"

"Aurora Hawthorn."

Professor Colt peered at me over the top of his glasses. "The lost cousin, right?"

"Uh..." How had my family's old nickname for me made its way all the way over here? "Not currently lost. Though this place is a bit of a maze."

He chuckled. "That it is. Can I help you with something?"

"You borrowed a book from our library a couple of weeks ago."

"Oh, yes, I have the date marked down," he said. "It's due to be returned in two days, right?"

"Right. But my aunt wondered if you'd be willing to return it early," I said. "We need the information in the book for something urgent."

"That's intriguing," he said. "Is Mr Bennet refusing to help with breaking a curse, by any chance?"

"Not exactly." Unless you counted not giving us the evidence we needed, but it was far too late to stop the curse when it'd already claimed its victim. "We're more trying to trace the origin of a curse than break one."

"Ah, that's even harder." He stepped out from behind the cabinet. "Not *impossible*. I prefer not to speak in such absolutes, and all kinds of magic are capable of things one might call impossible... depending on the limits of your imagination, that is. Take that library, for instance."

"What about it?" I asked, unsure what he was getting at.

"The library is the product of a curse which took on a life of its own, is it not?" he said. "A living and breathing example of 'theoretical'... in a manner of speaking."

I didn't know about 'living and breathing', but the library was certainly unique even in the magical world. "Do you come to the library often?"

"As often as I can get away from work." He chuckled. "I taught your father as a student, did you know? Your aunt Candace too. Adelaide, though, she preferred to study practical applications of magic. Her daughter is the same."

He'd taught my dad? "Really?"

"You look shocked." He gave another laugh. "Yes, I am that old. I remember when the library was new, and I have to admit I always hoped to study it myself. I understand why Adelaide keeps her mother's secrets locked up tight, though, and I respect that choice."

"You'd want to study the library for purely theoretical reasons?" I found myself wondering if his theoretical interest in curses extended to practical application, but did that extend to lethal creations which caused someone to drop dead? He looked like the mild-mannered professor type, hardly the sort to commit a cold-hearted murder, but looks could be deceiving. I'd learned that lesson in the magical world countless times already.

"Of course," he said. "Think how many new spells might be possible with the knowledge within the library's walls. Imagine the possibilities. Why, the books alone..."

Getting the distinct impression he was ready to go on a rant like Aunt Candace when she landed on a subject that she had a particular passion for, I cleared my throat. "Ah... can I have the book back?"

"Right, I forgot." He rapped on a door at the back of the room, hidden among the dusty filing cabinets. "Lara?"

A younger woman popped her head out of the back room. Really young, in fact—too much so to be an undergrad. "What is it, professor?"

"Lara, can you find the book I borrowed from the library?" he asked. "Aurora here needs it back."

"Oh, sure." She eyed me with evident surprise. "You're one of the Hawthorns, right? The new one?"

"I'm Aurora—Rory, usually," I said. "I work at the library. Um, are you a student here?"

"Lara is here on a scholarship," Professor Colt said fondly. "She's only sixteen, but she was leagues ahead of the academy students and is already applying for a PhD."

"Wow." And here I was, contemplating spending years before I caught up with the average witch, even taking into account my accelerated lessons. Let alone mastering the library's magic, which was a whole other entity in itself.

"Yeah, I'm pretty sure I've run into your cousin a few

times." She popped a piece of gum in her mouth and chewed. "Estelle, right?"

"Yeah, she's working on her thesis at the moment."

"Oh, really?" Her eyes brightened. "Do you think she'd mind if I asked her some questions?"

"I'm sure that won't be a problem," I said. "Just drop by the library at any time."

"I'll do that," she said. "Must be handy having all that knowledge at your fingertips."

I gave a nod. "Yeah. I'm still learning my way around it all."

"Right. You're new to the magical world," she said. "How's it been?"

"I'm coping." I'd been learning fast, actually, but recent events reminded me how little I really knew. "The book?"

"Right, of course." She ducked into the back room, from which a series of thuds ensued.

"What's in there?" I asked.

"Mostly spare books," the professor said. "I've worked here for long enough that I've amassed quite the collection. Magical theory is ever changing, after all."

Lara returned with a faded leather textbook, which she handed me.

"Thanks." I put the book into my shoulder bag and addressed the professor. "I'm sure it won't be long before we're finished with the book if you'd like to borrow it again. Feel free to come to the library too."

"I may peruse the rest of your collection while I'm there," he said. "If you ever develop an interest in academia, you're more than welcome to apply to the university."

"There's no age limit," Lara added. "It's never too late to learn."

From the slightly pitying look on her face, I might have been the professor's age, not twenty-five. I already had a stack of unpaid student loans from the regular world and didn't need to add any more, but I couldn't deny the idea held a certain appeal. I might have applied to do a PhD myself if not for the fact that I hadn't been able to justify leaving my dad's shop.

"Exactly," said Professor Colt. "Everything starts as an idea before it becomes reality. You should know that given your family's expertise, right?"

True. My family's magic could make the impossible real and could bring words to life... though I didn't think there was any kind of biblio-witchery which could do anything as vindictive as causing someone to drop dead on the spot.

"Sure," I said. "Thanks for the book."

I left the office and returned to Xavier's side, where he waited in the corridor. "Hey, Rory. Did you get the book?"

"I did," I said. "I'm pretty sure Professor Colt just offered to mentor me if I ever want to go into magical academia too."

"I can see you being happy in that kind of setting," he said. "If it's what you want to do, that is."

"Estelle's thesis is putting me off at the moment, to tell you the truth," I said. "Besides, I'm going to take years to catch up with the basics, let alone advanced magic."

All the same, as we left the building to return to the library, I entertained a little fantasy of having a private magical research office of my own.

6

The rest of the day passed fairly quickly. I took over the desk from Aunt Adelaide while she went to drop the book off at the hospital, but during a lull in visitors, I picked up the journal and resumed my painstaking progress of translating the various passages about my dad's continued adventures in Europe. Nevertheless, the interruptions were constant, and since Estelle remained as reclusive as Aunt Candace, I had to keep rushing to fetch books or shouting instructions to Jet and Sylvester.

Still, it was all worth it when Xavier came to pick me up for our date that evening at the end of my shift.

"Hey." He greeted me with a kiss. "Ready for our date?"

"Sure," I said. "We're going to the Black Dog pub, right?"

"Actually, I thought we might get takeout and head back to the Reaper's house."

Wait. He couldn't be serious, surely. "You want me to come over to your house?"

"I haven't given you a tour of the place yet, have I?"

"Considering your boss strictly forbade it, no." My heart began to beat faster. "Better hope he doesn't make a sudden appearance."

"He didn't strictly forbid me from inviting you over," he said. "Not in so many words. How about it?"

"You think I'd say no?" I grinned.

We picked up fish and chips before heading towards the cemetery, hand in hand. The gravestones were awash in darkness with no sources of light, natural or otherwise. Xavier pushed open the rusty iron gate and led the way in, at which point I tripped over someone very solid and very much alive.

"Ah!" I released Xavier's hand, squinting down at our unwelcome visitor. "What are you doing here?"

Nero the Wonder leapt to his feet, his bright hair the only splash of colour against the dark graveyard. "Reaper!"

Several of his companions popped up out of the shadows, including the girl whose pink hair matched his own. It seemed they'd been sitting behind the gate, waiting to ambush us.

"What exactly are you doing here?" Xavier demanded, putting on his scariest Reaper tone.

Nero barely blinked. "We're having a graveyard party."

"Seriously?" I spotted several bottles of some kind of cheap alcoholic beverage sitting nearby and even a pair of speakers. "Couldn't you have picked literally anywhere else? You can't even see anything in here."

"It's got a great atmosphere, you get me?" He squinted at my face. "Why're *you* here?"

"I live here," Xavier answered. "How many people did you invite to this party?"

"This is the Grim Reaper's home," I added. "He doesn't appreciate trespassers."

"He's not around," said Nero the Wonder.

"But I am." Xavier loomed over them, his own scythe appearing in his hand in a flash of light. "Get out, and be sure to tell everyone who you invited that the party is cancelled."

Nero the Wonder gaped at him for a moment, stunned into silence for possibly the first time in his life. "Right, right, I'm going."

He elbowed the gate open while his entourage practically tripped over themselves in an effort to follow him, vacating the cemetery in seconds.

Xavier shook his head after them. "Does he have a death wish?"

"Apparently," I murmured. "How did he know the Grim Reaper isn't around?"

He didn't know the cause of the Grim Reaper's disappearance, did he? He wasn't even from Ivory Beach, but his choice of party locations was dodgy to say the least.

"It's lucky for our pink-haired friend that he isn't." Xavier led me to the Grim Reaper's home, which resembled an average-sized detached house that sat alone at the back of the cemetery. He unlocked the front door and beckoned me inside.

While this wasn't my first visit, I'd only ever seen inside the room on the left of the hallway, which contained little more than a long wooden table surrounded by ancient, uncomfortable-looking chairs. I assumed that was the room the Grim Reaper used to meet with guests on the rare occasion that anyone paid him a visit. With the lights off, every shadow seemed to contain the Grim Reaper. Maybe this wasn't such a good idea after all.

I fixed my attention on Xavier. "Can you give me the tour? Of the public areas of the house, I mean."

"None of it is public, technically, but the ground floor is all fairly straightforward," he said. "That's the boss's meeting room on your left. On the right are the kitchen and the sitting room."

"You have a kitchen? Why?"

"Because there was one here when we moved in, and my boss didn't see the need to renovate," he said. "There're a couple of bathrooms and bedrooms upstairs for the same reason."

Come to think of it, even a living room seemed redundant, since Reapers didn't actually need to sit down. Or sleep. Or occupy space in this world. The house was almost entirely bare of any kind of human touch. No pictures on the walls, the bare minimum of furniture, plain cream wallpaper peeling off at the edges, old grey carpets. And dust. Lots of dust.

Xavier carried the takeaway bags into the living room and turned on the light while I sat on the musty sofa and immediately broke into a coughing fit at the clouds of dust that rose from my seat.

"Sorry," he said. "I'd offer to clean up a bit, but if I did, the boss would guess I'd invited someone over."

"It's okay." I coughed again, shivering when a chill breeze swept in from the corridor. "Do you have a working fireplace?"

He dubiously glanced at the dust-coated mantelpiece on the far side of the room. "There's one over there, but I'm fairly sure it hasn't been used in decades."

"The Grim Reaper didn't always live here, then?" I opened the takeout bag on my lap, trying to make myself at home despite the lack of any remote sense of homeliness inside the house.

"No." He sat next to me, reached into the bag, and pulled out a handful of chips. "But I've lived here throughout my entire apprenticeship."

Not for the first time, I wondered how long he'd been apprenticed to the Grim Reaper. Like vampires, Reapers stopped ageing when they decided to become a Reaper, so he might be a lot older than he looked. Or he might have been trained since childhood. He'd never dropped any hints as to his former life, after all.

We ate the fish and chips in companionable silence, and I did my level best not to drop any crumbs on the furniture. Not that you could see much for the dust. I hadn't been aware of how comparatively loud the library was, even at its quietest moments. There were always people around, and if not, the books filled the background with a faint whispering. The Grim Reaper's entire house was as silent as the grave.

"This doesn't seem like a nice place to grow up," I murmured. "How old were you when you moved here?"

"I don't want to keep secrets from you, Rory." He took my hand in his. "I'm treading a thin line between sharing what I can and not getting either of us into trouble. Especially you. When Reapers share their secrets with non-Reapers... the consequences can be severe."

Despite the warmth of his touch, I shivered. "Severe how?"

"If a Reaper chooses a non-Reaper as a partner, the easiest way to avoid punishment is for them to leave the Reaper fold altogether," he said. "They go back to living as a human. The problem is that there's no way to sever ties with the Reaper Council altogether. They keep tabs on all of us."

"That seems unfair."

"Reapers work in the intersection between the magical and non-magical worlds and interact with both. It's not fairness that drives our rules but secrecy. Our position allows us access to a certain type of magic which most of the paranormal world is not privy to. It doesn't make us very popular, so we hold ourselves apart by necessity."

"How do you get chosen as a Reaper, then?" I asked. "Does it run in the family?"

"Sometimes," he said. "We don't exactly advertise any open positions; otherwise, we'd get endless applications to join the fold. However, the Reaper Council is always keeping a watch on potential recruits and approaches them if they believe they'd be a good fit."

"I guess it's easier for them to watch relatives of living Reapers, right?"

"Reapers aren't living." His gaze dropped to the grey carpet. "We can't reproduce with one another, so any new recruits have to be gathered from among the general population. Or from the offspring of Reapers who broke the rules."

My brow furrowed. "So you aren't allowed relationships with non-Reapers, but the only way to find new Reapers is for someone to break the rules?"

"Reapers are immortal, Rory," he said. "They rarely *need* to be replaced. Also, I'm fairly sure I just broke several of my secrecy agreements by telling you that."

"Sorry," I said. "I can't help asking questions. I mean, it's relevant, right? To us, I mean."

"Yes." Sadness entered his gaze when he briefly met my eyes. "It is."

We could theoretically have children together if we didn't mind throwing the Reaper Council's rules out the window, but we couldn't marry. We couldn't live together. And if the Reaper Council saw fit to intervene, our entire relationship could come to a crashing halt, and we'd never be able to see one another again.

My eyes stung. This all seemed bitterly unfair, but who was I to ask him to give up his life's calling? Or rather, *after*life's calling, as the case may be?

I swallowed. "So you never had a choice, right? When you signed up, I mean?"

"No." He exhaled in a sigh. "No, and if I had to go back and make the choice again, it might have been different."

My heart skipped a beat. "How?"

I jumped violently when the doorbell rang. Every nerve in my body stood on end while Xavier swore under his breath.

"It's not him," I whispered. "He wouldn't ring the doorbell of his own house."

"No, but only one person regularly pays him visits in person."

"Evangeline."

Great. I should have known she'd find out about his absence, but how? Had she been roaming around and picked it up through combing the minds of one of Nero the Wonder's friends who we'd kicked out of the cemetery? Or maybe she'd got into Laney's thoughts or even come to the conclusion on her own. She was too clever by half, and too persistent.

Xavier strode down the hall to open the door, and as I'd feared, Evangeline stood there on the doorstep, looking as stunning as ever. "Ah, Reaper. Is that Aurora too?"

I didn't see much point in hiding myself, so I stepped up to his side. "Yes, I'm here. Is there a reason you came to disturb us?"

"I simply wanted to visit your boss," she said. "Is he not in?"

"Not at the moment," said Xavier while I did my best to keep my thoughts blank so she wouldn't be able to draw any more clues from my mind.

"Pity," said Evangeline. "I wonder what was important enough for him to risk leaving his apprentice behind."

"Who said anything about a risk?" I kept my attention on a crack in the wallpaper to keep from letting any unwanted thoughts slip out.

Evangeline merely smiled. "I do hope he isn't gone for long. I enjoy our meetings, I have to admit, despite our differing perspectives. I suppose his absence does present opportunities for the two of you, but it must be a little concerning."

She knows. But had she seen to his disappearance herself?

"What my boss is doing is none of your concern whatsoever," Xavier told Evangeline, his pleasant tone surprisingly chilling. I'd never seen him directly stand up to the head vampire before, but with his boss gone, *he* was the leading Reaper in town and the person in charge of protecting their all-important secrets. "If you want to speak to him, then you're welcome to come back at a later date unless I can help you with something myself."

"Oh, it's of no import," she said. "We've had our differences, but I do admire his dedication to his job. I find teaching youngsters can be rewarding myself. Like your friend, for instance, Aurora. Did Laney tell you she bit a human for the first time yesterday?"

Her words rang through my mind. "She *what?*"

"She didn't tell you." A smile curled her lip. "I expect she would rather have preserved her innocence in your eyes, but she isn't the friend you once knew."

My nails dug into my palms. "Laney is who she says she is. Not who *you* say she is."

"I never suggested otherwise." She stepped away from the house. "I will see you both soon, I'm sure."

Evangeline departed with the swiftness of a vampire, and I jumped when Xavier put a hand on my shoulder. "Ignore her, Rory."

"Little difficult." I couldn't seem to stop shivering. "Laney *bit* someone. I should have checked in with her yesterday, but I was busy with the poetry night."

"I'm sure your family would have noticed if there was a problem," he said.

"They might not have." Estelle had been holed up working on her essay, Aunt Adelaide had been out for most of the day, and the others paid zero attention to my best friend.

"I'm sure she was just taunting you," he said. "You know she's a manipulator."

"Yeah, which makes me worried about what she might

end up doing now she knows the Grim Reaper isn't around."

"She does whatever she wants anyway," said Xavier. "It'll be fine, Rory."

I hoped he was right. I also felt bad about leaving him, but the mood was ruined, and worry for Laney would gnaw at me until I was sure she was okay. Besides, I *shouldn't* be here. If the Grim Reaper came back, or if he had the faintest inkling how many of the Reapers' secrets I'd learned, then Xavier would face worse consequences than me.

Xavier walked me back to the library without objection, and I gave him a long kiss goodbye as an apology and to make it clear I didn't blame *him* for the vampire leader's meddling.

As I entered the building, Laney appeared in my line of sight, crossing the lobby with the typical grace of one of the vampires. I immediately tensed at the sight of her. "Laney."

"Hey, Rory," she said. "Weren't you with Xavier?"

"I was until a certain vampire leader showed up at his house."

Her eyes widened. "Why'd she visit him?"

"She said you bit someone." I searched her face. "Are you okay?"

"I think you're supposed to ask if the other person is okay." She gave a shaky laugh. "Which she is. I wanted to see if I could control my bloodlust, and she agreed to be a guinea pig."

I blinked. "You mean you grabbed a random person off the street and asked if she wanted to be bitten?"

She gave an eye roll. "No. The vamps held a party, and non-vamps were invited too. Don't look at me like that, Rory. It wasn't anything like the Founders' events."

Goosebumps prickled my arms. "I hope it wasn't, because last time didn't end so well."

"I can't get turned into a vampire twice, can I?" She gave a smile. "Don't worry about me, Rory. I know what I'm doing."

"Did Evangeline mention why she likes to have the occasional chat with the Grim Reaper?" I asked.

"Because they're both misanthropic immortals?" Laney suggested. "No clue. Did you ask *him?*"

I hesitated, then I figured she'd end up finding out soon enough, given that the one person guaranteed to read her thoughts already knew. "The Grim Reaper disappeared the same night as the murder. Xavier hasn't heard from him since then, but Evangeline has figured it out. Don't ask me how."

Unless she'd caused it herself, a theory I couldn't entirely dismiss.

Laney's eyes rounded. "How's it possible for him to disappear?"

"Believe me, I'm lost too," I said. "But Evangeline is going to use this situation to her advantage."

"To do what?" asked Laney. "Don't get me wrong, I know she's a creepy manipulator, but it's not like she can move into his house and steal his scythe or anything."

"I guess not." That mental image was mildly amusing, but it didn't quell my unease. "The way she referred to him not being around made it sound like she knew more even than Xavier did, which isn't right."

"I can ask some questions at our next lesson," she said.

"I'd rather you didn't put yourself at risk." Laney was new enough to being a vampire that most things which would scare normal people gave her a buzz, but her vamp status didn't make her immune from retaliation at Evangeline's hands if she annoyed her enough.

"I'm not," said Laney. "Trust me. I don't need to be able to read her mind to get answers from her. She likes to talk to me."

"Laney, that really isn't a good thing," I said. "She wants you to entrust her with your secrets... and mine too."

Specifically, the journal. While I'd started to piece together when the animosity between my dad and the vampires had begun, I had yet to uncover anything which would have been valuable and interesting to the head vampire. Yet.

Laney's brow furrowed. "I get why you're wary of her, Rory, but it'd be nice if you had more faith in me than that."

"I do," I said. "Sorry if I sounded like I didn't. The Grim Reaper being missing is screwing with my head, to be honest, and Evangeline showing up at his house didn't help at all."

"I get it," said Laney. "Look, I'm fine. It's all under control."

I didn't argue. I knew better. "Okay. I just worry about you."

Movement stirred nearby, and she shifted on the balls of her feet. "See you later, okay?"

While she returned to the living quarters, I spotted

Cass watching from the shadow of a nearby bookshelf and almost jumped out of my skin.

"How long have you been standing there?" I asked. "You could give a vampire a run for their money in stealth."

"Maybe you're just unobservant," she said. "Your friend is right."

"About what?" For some reason, she refused to refer to Laney by her name despite the fact that she'd been living here in the library for weeks by this point. It'd taken less time for her to warm to *me,* and she'd done her level best to drive me out of the library at first, so I didn't know what it'd take to make her view Laney as anything other than an intruder.

"Let her do what she likes," said Cass. "If she wants to go to vampire parties and bite willing humans, let her live her life. Or undeath, if you like."

"Do you see me stopping her?" I asked. "I only reminded her of Evangeline being a manipulator because sometimes *I* forget that."

"Which makes it your problem."

"Cass, you know perfectly well that any problem that affects Laney or me might rebound on the rest of us. Especially where Evangeline is concerned."

"The Founders are in jail," she said. "Laney is learning to be a bloodsucker, and I assume flirting with the head vampire is a novelty. Let her get it out of her system."

"I *hope* that's not what's going on." I shuddered. "Evangeline is centuries older than her and creepy on a good day."

No, she wasn't trying to flirt with her, but trying to

outmanoeuvre someone who had centuries of experience on her was bound to end in disaster.

"What about the rest of it?" she asked.

"You mean the Grim Reaper being walkabout and Evangeline knowing more than anyone else?" I asked. "Does that not concern you a little?"

"I can see why you and Xavier are drawn together. You're both great at worrying over nothing at all."

"Thanks?" I shook my head. "I wouldn't call the Grim Reaper 'nothing'. Xavier told me he'd never dropped off the radar like that before. And he visited the curse-breaker right before his disappearance."

"That means he's probably out of town on business," she said. "Chill. You should be having fun with Xavier, not worrying about his boss. You didn't even ask to see his room, did you?"

Heat crept up my neck. "If I didn't know better, I'd ask if you were planning to attend Nero the Wonder's grave-yard party and were hiding there all the time."

Cass's brows shot up. "A party in a graveyard?"

"Xavier and I had to chase his whole entourage out of the graveyard," I said. "Pity Evangeline didn't run into *them*."

"Tell Aunt Candace so she can use that one in a book," said Cass. "Weirdos."

Weirdos… or potential murderers. I couldn't picture any of them driving off the Grim Reaper given how they'd reacted to Xavier's scythe, but maybe that'd been an act.

As for Cass, she might as well have been able to read my thoughts herself, but maybe she was right about Laney. She was capable of making her own decisions, reckless newbie vampire or not.

Xavier, though… we didn't exactly have a conventional relationship, but would he be willing to give away his apprenticeship to be with me in a more long-term manner? With the Grim Reaper gone, that option was off the table for the time being, since if Xavier was the main Reaper for the area, quitting wouldn't be an option.

I could hardly believe I wanted the Grim Reaper to come back, but I genuinely did.

7

I woke the following morning to the sound of
Sylvester singing in my ear. With a groan, I pulled
the bedcovers over my head. "Don't you have
anyone else to annoy?"

"No. Estelle locked me out of her room."

I let the covers fall back. "Did she now?"

I'd have to ask for the details when I next saw her,
because Aunt Candace had shut down my attempts to
find out how to owl-proof my room. Shooing him away, I
went to shower and dress before heading downstairs to
grab breakfast. I found the kitchen deserted, but someone
had left out a plate of toast and some coffee, presumably
Aunt Adelaide. I wondered if she'd gone back to the
hospital again, but with nobody else around, I figured I
might as well steal a few moments to work on translating
my dad's journal. I hadn't had the chance to pick it up
yesterday, and my focus had been lacking after my interrupted visit to Xavier's house, but it'd lurked in the back
of my mind ever since.

Unfortunately, I'd hardly opened the journal before Sylvester swooped into the kitchen and sat on the table. "Getting exciting, is it? Unearthed any tantalising secrets?"

I bit into my toast instead. "Considering I'm moving at the pace of a snail, I'll be lucky if I finish this century."

"That's insulting to snails," said the owl.

I rolled my eyes. "You know, the way you're happy to leave Estelle alone to work on her thesis proves you *are* capable of giving us space if we really want it."

"You have plenty of space." He spread his wings wide and nearly knocked over my coffee mug. "See?"

"You know that isn't what I meant." I snatched the journal out of the way before the owl spilled coffee all over it. "I can't focus with you hovering around in the background. Unless you have anything useful you wanted to share?"

"And what would be worthy of your attention?" he enquired.

I took another bite and considered his question while chewing. "Would the Forbidden Room be able to tell me how a curse might cause someone to drop dead?"

"There is nothing the Room does not know," he said.

I returned to my toast. "That doesn't explain whether or not it'll actually be able to give me an answer."

"That would defeat the purpose, wouldn't it?"

"What purpose?"

"Annoying you." The owl took flight again, forcing me to move my coffee out of range of his wings. Resigning myself to another wasted opportunity, I returned the journal to my bag and finished my toast before Sylvester decided to snatch it from my plate.

"You're a menace, you are." I swatted him away from my coffee. "Maybe I'll ask the Book of Questions how to make you a cage."

"There is no cage that can hold me," the owl announced. "*Him,* on the other hand…"

I looked to see who he was referring to, and Jet zipped into view like a feathery ball of energy. "Partner, he's outside!"

"Who's outside?" I asked the crow.

"The Reaper."

Hoping he meant Xavier and not the *other* Reaper—even if his return would have solved at least one of our current problems—I followed Jet to the front door and pushed it open. Sure enough, Xavier stood on the doorstep, his blond curls lifting in the cold breeze. A flush came to my face as I recalled the previous evening, but his grave expression hinted that he wasn't here to pick up where we'd left off.

"What's going on?" I asked.

He drew in a breath. "I didn't want to worry you, but I was called out to pick up another soul last night."

"Who?" My heart dropped. "Anyone we know?"

"I think your aunt might know him," he said. "The person who died was at the hospital, working the night shift. When I went to Reap his soul, he had no idea he was dead."

Oh no. "From the curse?"

"I asked if he remembered how he died," said Xavier. "He didn't. It sounds like he simply dropped dead out of nowhere, the same as Rufus did."

"That's bizarre." And suspicious. "You think he might

have figured out something about the curse, and the person responsible wanted to take him out?"

"I didn't ask," he said. "Perhaps I should have, but he was in shock over being dead, and it seemed unlikely that he knew he'd been hit by a curse at all."

Regardless, if the same curse had killed both victims, it was a safe bet that the perpetrator was the same person as well, but it was hard to draw any other conclusions when I hadn't met the victim myself. I might have witnessed Xavier taking his soul to the afterlife if I'd stayed at his house, admittedly, but that didn't necessarily mean I'd have found out anything substantial.

Given that both victims had been hit by a curse without even knowing, we might as well be dealing with an invisible killer.

"I didn't mean to freak you out," he added. "Is your family not around?"

"I assume Aunt Adelaide is at the hospital again," I said. "Not sure if she knew the victim, but there's a good chance they ran into one another at some point in the last day or so."

"I hope they get to the bottom of it, then," he said. "Also, I never asked... how is Laney?"

Oh. Right. "She's fine. Or she says she is."

Laney's apparently rejuvenated interest in vampire parties was a whole other issue, and I didn't know how much of my apprehension about her situation was justified. Especially when it'd been a vampire party which had ultimately sealed her fate and cut her off from the regular world.

Xavier studied my face. "But you don't think she is?"

"You mean about the biting-people thing?" I asked.

"She says it was consensual, but she's also apparently been going to vampire-run parties. Even... even after the outcome of the last one."

His eyes widened a fraction. "That's her choice, but I can understand why you're worried about her."

"You don't think I'm being too much of a control freak?" I asked. "Cass does."

"Since when was Cass an expert on having your ordinary best friend turned into a vampire?" Xavier said. "She doesn't understand."

No, and she doesn't understand what it's like to be dating the Reaper, either. "Maybe not, but Laney seems to agree with her. She also thinks she has nothing to fear from Evangeline."

"I think that might be her newbie vampire confidence talking," said Xavier. "I imagine Evangeline is doing her best to seem nonthreatening to her."

"Because she wants to gain her trust." I shuddered. "I know Laney is stronger than she used to be, but Evangeline can pluck any thought from her head whenever she feels like it, and being immortal doesn't make her immune to her trickery. I don't like that Evangeline knows the Grim Reaper has gone walkabout, either."

"Neither do I," he said. "From what she said last night, I gathered she worked it out for herself rather than reading it from anyone's thoughts, but that doesn't mean she doesn't stand to gain anything from his absence."

"Exactly," I said. "I never told Laney or anyone he was missing, just in case, but she's smart enough to have drawn her own conclusions."

Footsteps sounded behind me, and Xavier glanced over my shoulder. "Your cousin's here."

"I should tell her about the second murder," I said. "See you later?"

"Of course." He left after planting a kiss on my mouth while I found a sleepy-looking Estelle hovering in the entryway to our family's living quarters.

"Hey," I said. "Another late night?"

"Yeah." She yawned. "I slept right through the messages Mum left me. Why's she at the hospital again?"

"Someone else died. One of the staff members, I think."

Worry furrowed her brow. "Oh no."

"Xavier just told me," I said. "He said the guy more or less just dropped dead out of nowhere. No idea who did it."

"So it's the same curse?" Estelle paled. "I guess that's why she went back. That's horrible."

"I know." The urge hit me to try asking the Book of Questions about the curse after all, but with the mood Sylvester was in, it was anyone's guess as to whether he'd give me a straight answer. "How's the essay?"

She pulled a face. "I'm through the worst of it, I think, but it's hard to say how much longer I'll need."

"I'll take over at the front desk today," I said. "It's no bother."

"Thanks, Rory." Her gaze went to the translator document sticking out of my bag. "Were you working on the journal?"

"Before Sylvester interrupted," I said. "On that note, how'd you lock Sylvester out of your room? I thought he could get into any room in the library regardless of whether it was locked or not."

"He can," she said. "Which is really annoying. I use a

freezing spell on the door instead of a locking spell, and it seemed to work. Have you learned that one yet?"

"No, I haven't."

"I can teach you." She crossed the lobby towards the Reading Corner. "The problem is that if you let the ice melt afterwards, it's a nightmare to clean up. Worth it for a little peace, though."

"Yeah, it'd be nice to have the occasional morning's lie-in without an owl alarm clock waking me up."

She glanced at me, a teasing smile playing on her mouth. "I thought you wanted peace to work on the journal, but I guess the Grim Reaper's house can't be a nice place for a sleepover. I doubt freezing the door would stop him walking in on you and his apprentice, either."

"Uh…" I might have mentioned it'd been Evangeline who'd interrupted yesterday evening, but I'd prefer to put the vampires *and* the Grim Reaper out of mind for the time being. "I do want the occasional hour to translate the journal in peace. Sylvester almost spilled coffee all over it earlier."

"What a nuisance." She reached one of the classroom doors near the Reading Corner. "We can practise here."

"All right." While she shut the door, I pulled out my notebook and the pen which enabled me to access my family's unique magic. "Which word do I write?"

"*Freeze.*"

"Got it." I flipped to a clean page and pressed the point of the pen to the paper, feeling the flow of magic to the ink in my pen as I focused my attention on the door. Then I wrote the word *Freeze*.

At once, ice flowed from my hands and filled the gap

between the door and the wall. Estelle reached for the handle and pulled, but the door stuck fast. "Nice job."

"Good," I said. "How do I get rid of it without causing a flood?"

"Cross out the word," she said. "No need to start any fires."

"Definitely not in my plan." I scribbled out the word, and to my relief, the ice disappeared from the doorway. "Useful one to know. Thanks."

"No worries," she said. "Though Sylvester might figure out a way around the spell if you use it on him too often. Fair warning."

"Good to know." If I annoyed him too much, he might ban me from the Forbidden Room too. While I didn't have any faith in the Book of Questions to help us pin down the elusive killer, I'd better save the owl-proofing until we'd found the culprit behind the curse.

As Estelle and I returned to the front desk, Aunt Adelaide came back into the library, her hair windswept. "Hey, Rory. Oh, you're out of your room, Estelle."

"Everything okay?" Estelle asked. "I heard about someone dying at the hospital. Rory told me."

"Yes, it happened right after I left." She turned to me. "How did you—right, Xavier."

"Yeah, he dropped by the library to tell me," I said. "Was it the same curse as before?"

"It looked that way." She released a sigh. "Again, the victim had no obvious enemies. The only possibility was that he was on the trail of Rufus's killer, but if he was, he didn't tell any of his colleagues."

"Do the police think the two cases are connected?" Estelle asked.

"Not officially yet, but given the cause of death, it's hard to imagine two different culprits," said Aunt Adelaide. "I went to speak to Edwin on the way back, but he admitted that two dead bodies with no obvious cause makes it hard to convict anyone."

"There must be something," I said. "Do you think the curse was put on him at the hospital? By someone else who works there?"

"Everyone in that department has openly shared all they know of illegal curses while trying to figure out the cause of Rufus's death," she said. "None of them was acquainted with Rufus, either, before his body was found. There's nothing to link the pair of them save for the cause of death. Did Xavier see anything odd when he took the second victim's soul into the afterlife?"

"No," I said. "The victim didn't know he was dead. Same as Rufus. I did wonder if he found out who killed Rufus, and the murderer targeted him next."

"If he did, he kept the knowledge to himself," she said. "The other staff are stunned. They'd barely begun to make progress, but they were operating on the assumption that the killer had a grudge against Rufus in particular."

"But they still think the curse was a new one?" I asked. "Not on record, or whatever it was you said?"

"Yes," she said. "I know Mr Bennet insists that he can only help with *breaking* curses, but really, we could use a little direction. He can't be entirely ignorant on the subject."

Guilt twisted a knot in my chest. With the turmoil of the past day, I'd utterly forgotten the minor secret I hadn't told the rest of my family. "Aunt Adelaide, there's something you should know. The Grim Reaper is missing. He disappeared the night of the first murder."

"He did?" Aunt Adelaide stared at me. "That can't be right."

"The Grim Reaper can't be *missing*," said Estelle. "Can he?"

"Even Xavier can't find him," I said. "And—the last person to see him was the curse-breaker."

Aunt Adelaide's expression shadowed. "Xavier told you that?"

"Mr Bennet told us he saw the Grim Reaper not long after he escorted Rufus's soul into the afterlife," I explained. "Unfortunately, Mr Bennet refused to tell us what they discussed, and the Grim Reaper has yet to return."

"How typical of him," said Aunt Adelaide. "The Grim Reaper, though… Estelle is right. It's not possible for him to simply vanish."

"You think the Grim Reaper might have known about the curse?" Estelle asked.

"I can't think why else he'd have visited Mr Bennet," I said. "He *said* Rufus had no idea he'd been murdered, but maybe he picked up on something from the crime scene that the rest of us didn't. Even Xavier."

"So he went to the curse-breaker," Aunt Adelaide said. "Then he disappeared."

"I doubt the murderer made the *Grim Reaper* disappear, though," said Estelle. "Aren't Reapers supposed to be more or less immune to curses?"

"Probably," I said. "Why can't Xavier track him down, though? Usually, he can use his Reaper senses to find him, but he told me he hasn't been able to detect a trace of him. It's hard not to suspect some kind of foul play."

"Didn't the two of them have a disagreement?" Aunt Adelaide said. "You mentioned the Grim Reaper was unhappy with Xavier's recent decisions, didn't you? I'm sure he's capable of preventing his apprentice from finding him if he so desires."

"You mean he might have been in town the whole time?" Alarm flooded me. If he was still in Ivory Beach, then he'd know Xavier had let me into his house. He might even know that Xavier had told me secrets no non-Reaper was supposed to know.

Aunt Adelaide must have seen the fear on my face. "If he *is* nearby, I doubt he's watching his apprentice closely. Otherwise he wouldn't have gone to such lengths not to be followed."

I shook my head. "Then he's asking for trouble. Evangeline knows he's missing, and I'm sure she'll be out to take advantage of him not being here."

"By doing what?" Estelle asked. "I understand why you're worried, Rory, but Evangeline does whatever she likes regardless of what anyone thinks. Including the Grim Reaper."

"He did at least keep her in check," I said. "Kind of."

"I can guarantee the Grim Reaper would reappear if she stepped too far out of line," added Aunt Adelaide.

"You mean if she threw a party in the graveyard?" I asked. "Because Nero the Wonder tried that, and Xavier had to throw him out."

Really, *that* ought to have proven if Grim Reaper had been around, since he'd have turfed Nero the Wonder and his entire entourage out. Right?

"What did he do that for?" Estelle's brow wrinkled. "A graveyard party? Really?"

"That's what he said he was doing there," I said. "Not sure if he might have had ulterior motives. He *is* new in town, but I don't see him cursing anyone."

Estelle shook her head. "He's not that subtle. Anyway, it's almost opening time, but I need to get back to my thesis before Sylvester finds a way around the spell I put on my room."

"I can take over the front desk," said Aunt Adelaide. "I'm staying here for the time being, unless Edwin or the staff at the hospital want me to come back."

"I hope they remember to return the books they borrowed." My gaze went to the clock, which had just gone nine, and then to the window, where I glimpsed a shock of bright-pink hair. "Oh, no."

The door swung open a moment later. I suppressed a groan when Nero the Wonder entered the library, swaggering into the lobby as if he was walking into his own personal hotel suite. His entourage followed, while Estelle made a hasty retreat. I didn't blame her a bit.

"Hey." Nero the Wonder snapped his fingers at me as if calling for room service or summoning a servant. "You work here, right? Show me around."

He had to be joking. Hadn't he seen enough of the library on Monday evening's poetry night? "Is there anything in particular you're looking for?"

He shrugged. "I dunno. I just feel like a change of scenery, you get me?"

"I can give you an abbreviated tour of the ground floor, then." I'd have preferred a 'please', but if he had anything else to say on the matter of yesterday's attempted graveyard party, now was the time for me to ask.

Aunt Adelaide gave me a questioning look, but I returned it with a nod to indicate I had a plan. Though with his entourage practically glued to his side at all times, questioning him alone would take some finesse.

I started by pointing out the research section and the Reading Corner, giving everyone the chance to do their own exploration. While they lost themselves in the maze of shelves, I snagged my chance to talk to Nero the Wonder alone.

"So you're thinking of moving here?" I asked.

"Yeah, I am," he said. "Great scenery for filming videos, you get me? Especially in here."

Okay, I needed to shut down *that* idea fast. "I'm pretty sure my aunt would object if you wanted to use the library as a backdrop for your videos. In fact, the library itself might object too."

"Huh?" He blinked. "It's a library. It can't think."

"I wouldn't say that where the library can hear you." Typically, Sylvester was absent when his penchant for making mischief would have come in handy, but I didn't need to give Nero the Wonder any new ideas. "Also, you can't throw a party in here either. Why'd you pick the graveyard? Did you really not know that's where the Grim Reaper lives?"

"Ah." Guilt slid into his expression, which instantly raised my suspicions.

"You knew he wasn't going to be there," I said. "Who told you? It definitely wasn't his apprentice."

"Does it matter?" He folded his arms. "Why were *you* with the Reaper's apprentice?"

"We're dating." I figured that would get his attention, and sure enough, he gawped at me.

"You… you're with *that?*" he spluttered. "How? Isn't he dead?"

That was a little uncalled for. "I'm not here to talk about my dating life. I'm here to ask why you trespassed in the Grim Reaper's territory. Xavier would like to know too. If you don't want an untimely visit from the Reaper, then you're better off telling me instead."

He backed up against the shelf, his eyes widening beneath his bright-pink hair. "There's no need for that. It wasn't anything serious."

"All I want to know is who told you the Grim Reaper wasn't there. I won't tell anyone else." Not necessarily true, but he wouldn't be in town forever, and the quicker I ruled him out as a suspect, the better.

He released a breath. "I went to visit the vampires to ask if I could film a video in front of their church."

I winced. "You asked *Evangeline?* What did she have to say to that?"

More to the point, how had he walked away on his own feet?

"She said the graveyard would be a better location to film a video," he said. "She added that the Grim Reaper was out of town, so it was the perfect opportunity."

Thanks for that, Evangeline. "Well, there's more than one Reaper."

"I know that now." He gave me a wary look. "You won't tell him?"

"No." I would, but Nero the Wonder didn't have to worry about any retaliation unless he made the same mistake again. While his confession had proved Evangeline's scheming knew no bounds, it also said nothing whatsoever about the Grim Reaper's disappearance.

I called Jet over as I left the Reading Corner and asked him to keep an eye on Nero's entourage before I went to join Aunt Adelaide at the front desk.

"Everything okay?" she asked.

I lowered my voice. "Turns out Evangeline was the one who told Nero that the Grim Reaper was out of town. That's why he was hanging out in the graveyard."

"Why would she do that?" Aunt Adelaide asked.

"Because the alternative was letting him film a video in her church," I said. "I know, it's weird. Anyway, it's proof that Evangeline is spreading word about the Grim Reaper's absence to anyone who stops by the church. You don't think *she* knows where he is?"

It would explain how she'd found out about his supposed disappearance, at the very least, but what reason would he possibly have for telling her and not his apprentice?

"At this point, it wouldn't surprise me," Aunt Adelaide remarked. "Did she see him leave, I wonder?"

"Either that or he told her," I said. "I'm starting to think this is some kind of test aimed at Xavier, to be honest."

"A test of loyalty, do you think?" She made a clucking noise with her teeth. "That doesn't imply a connection to either of the curse's victims, though."

"No, but Xavier can track his boss through some kind of sixth sense, and I bet the Grim Reaper does have a way to switch it off if he wants to."

Honestly, he and Evangeline were as bad as each other. You'd think they'd act a little more mature given that both were immortals who were centuries older than the rest of us, but their agelessness seemed to have eroded their sense of decorum. If the Grim Reaper had ever had any to begin with, that is.

Maybe Xavier and I should confront the vampires' leader directly and give the Grim Reaper a reason to show his face again, but was it worth ticking off Evangeline? I didn't know.

A sudden loud screech came from behind me. I spun on my heel, hearing shouting coming from Nero the Wonder's general direction, and Jet zipped past with an incoherent squawk. As I ran to ask what the problem was, Xavier appeared, in full Grim Reaper mode with his scythe out.

"Oh no." I halted, my gaze on the scythe. "Tell me you're not here to collect a soul."

"I'm sorry, Rory," he said. "Someone died in here."

8

I scarcely paused for breath as I hurried behind Xavier to the back of the library where I'd left Nero the Wonder and his friends. When I spotted the pink-haired victim lying on a beanbag, I thought Nero himself had fallen victim to the curse, but the victim turned out to be the girl who'd dyed her hair to match his. Xavier strode over to her, trailing darkness behind him.

The rest of the crowd backed away as shadows filled the Reading Corner, blanking out my surroundings until the library itself vanished to the corners of my vision. Within the darkness surrounding Xavier and the girl's body, a door appeared, only visible due to the faint glow outlining its edges.

Nearby, the ghostly figure of the teenage girl appeared, even her pink hair washed of all colour in the surrounding gloom. A bewildered expression appeared on her face when she saw Xavier. "Why is it all dark? Who are you?"

"I am the Reaper," said Xavier. "Do you remember how

you died?"

"Died?" She pressed a hand to her chest and let out a shriek when it passed straight through her ghostly form. "I can't be dead. Nero the Wonder! Come and save me!"

Nobody appeared. Of course, we were the only ones who could hear her—Xavier because he was the Reaper and me because since we'd started growing closer to one another, I'd gained the ability to see into the afterlife along with him. It'd freaked me out a bit at first, I wouldn't lie, but I was glad of that extra proof of our closeness.

Right now? Not so much. The girl's distress was horrible to witness, but there was nothing I could do to reassure her. She didn't even seem to see me, only Xavier, as he guided her through the glowing door and out of sight. The shadows folded back, revealing the rest of Nero the Wonder's horrified entourage.

"She's gone," Xavier told them. "Did anyone see what happened?"

"She just dropped dead," spluttered a pale wizard with red hair. "Out of nowhere. Is this place cursed?"

"Definitely not." My heart began to beat faster. Had they brought the curse in here with them? "Wait a second. I'll fetch my aunt."

Aunt Adelaide was already on her way to the back of the library, her phone in her hand. "Someone died? Who was it?"

"She called herself Nera," said Nero the Wonder. "She was one of my biggest fans. How can this have happened?"

"The Reaper took her!" The redheaded wizard pointed straight at Xavier.

"It's my job." Xavier's tone was measured. "She was already dead when I got here."

"She was only a kid," he argued. "It's not fair."

"I know." Aunt Adelaide stepped in to reassure them. "Rory, can you wait over by the desk? I called the hospital and Edwin, but I'm not sure who will show up first."

"What if whatever killed her is here in the library?" I whispered to Xavier. "Can curses move around?"

"If they're attached to an object? Yes, they can." His expression was as grim as his boss. "I think the rest of your family should know in case it's still here."

"Cass is up in her lair with the animals, and Aunt Candace is working on a book," I said. "And Estelle is up to her neck in her thesis. They might be safer not leaving their rooms, though."

I looked around as if a giant arrow would appear, pointing me in the right direction like one of Nero the Wonder's conjuring tricks, but the only thing flying around was a still-panicking Jet. Where was Sylvester?

"I doubt the curse is on the loose in here, but we need to know how it got into the library to begin with," Xavier said. "I don't want to step on Edwin's toes, but someone should talk to Nero the Wonder and his companions."

"I did find out it was Evangeline who sent them to the graveyard to film a video instead of using the church," I told him. "Doesn't explain why someone would put a curse on them, though."

Admittedly, Nero the Wonder's followers weren't exactly all there. Had one of them stumbled upon the curse, accidentally or otherwise? Or were they hiding a killer in their midst?

Estelle came running into view. "Rory, what's going—"

"Hang on," I said. "The curse hit someone else, and we're not sure if they brought it in here with them."

"How can they have brought the curse into the library?" She stared over my shoulder at the chaos unfolding in the Reading Corner. "What triggered it? Do you know?"

"No idea. She just dropped dead, and nobody seems to know why."

"I'll talk to my mum."

Estelle ran over to Aunt Adelaide while I made for the desk again. On the way, Aunt Candace came flying downstairs and into the lobby. "Where's the body?"

"Keep it down," I said. "How did you even know there was a body?"

"I hear things." Jet flew past her, shrieking. No doubt he'd alerted her attention. "Someone died in here and I missed it? Why does that always happen?"

"It's not all that exciting, and please keep it down." I glanced over at the door and spotted Lara from the university standing uncertainly in the entryway.

She threw her gum into the bin, looking sheepish. "Is this a bad time?"

Oops. If I had to guess, she'd come to speak to Estelle about her magical thesis. "There's been a death in here, a freak accident."

"Oh, that's awful."

"Yeah." I looked around for Estelle and saw her talking to Aunt Adelaide. "Can you come back later? I think we're going to be out of action for the next few hours."

"Oh, of course!" She hopped out the door and nearly got mowed down by one of Edwin's troll guards in the process.

Two trolls entered, followed by the elf policeman and several uniformed wizards and witches who I guessed had come from the hospital.

"Edwin." I hastened over to him, accompanied by Xavier. "The victim dropped dead out of nowhere, same as the others. The curse—"

"I will take care of it, Rory." He strode through the library with his troll guards in tow, followed by the staff from the hospital.

Xavier waylaid him on the way to the Reading Corner. "Edwin, we didn't see what triggered the curse, but we can only assume it came in with the victim or one of her companions."

"You don't need to remind me of the perils of handling curses, Reaper," said the elf policeman. "I thought the current assumption was that the person cursing people was doing so from a distance."

"This time, the curse claimed two people in the space of a day," I said. "They're moving faster."

Now would be a good time to have access to the library's collection of textbooks on curses, but from the looks of things, the hospital staff had left them behind. Then again, given that they'd lost one of their staff members last night, I didn't exactly blame them for being distracted. I approached a tired-looking wizard with Asian heritage who wore a harried expression as if he'd just run here from the hospital ward. "Excuse me. I wondered if you had the books my Aunt Adelaide loaned you and the other staff?"

"I'm afraid not," he said. "Truth be told, the most useful book we had was misplaced at some point in the past day, and we have yet to find it."

"Which book?" I had a feeling I knew precisely which he meant. "Was that the book Aunt Adelaide brought you most recently?"

"Yes, that's the one."

"I hope it shows up soon," I said. "Did you get anything useful from it, then? Any ideas as to how the curse is being passed around?"

"Everything is pure conjecture at this point, unfortunately," he said. "As for the curse, we worked out that it likely isn't being cast on each victim directly. It's more plausible that it was cast on an object instead."

"Then how would it have ended up in the hands of one of Nero the Wonder's followers?" That part, I didn't get. "Has he set foot in the hospital?"

"I'm afraid I don't know." He turned back to the other staff members. "Maybe ask them yourself."

Edwin's trolls barred the way to the Reading Corner, but Xavier gave me a concerned look. "Did he say the curse is being spread via an object?"

"He guessed it was, but unless Nero the Wonder was trying to film a video at the hospital, I don't know how it'd have spread from last night's victim to one of his followers."

And what object was it? If it's still in here... anyone might pick it up.

"I'll ask Edwin to mention that when he questions them." Xavier wove his way through the crowd towards the elf policeman, while I hovered in the background. I hoped the hospital staff had had enough experience with curses not to handle them with their bare hands, but it'd got the better of one of them already.

Xavier returned to my side. "Nobody is admitting to

going near the hospital, but it's hard to get a word in edgeways over there."

"Someone must have," I said. "It's the only way they might have come into contact with the curse."

"Exactly," said Xavier. "I can have a look around the hospital myself. I might need to use my Reaper powers to get in without being stopped, but I can take you with me if you like."

My mouth parted. That was definitely against the Reapers' rulebook. "Are you sure we won't get caught?"

"By whom?" he asked. "The staff won't stop me from walking around their corridors. As for the Grim Reaper, getting his attention at this point wouldn't be a bad thing."

"Fair point." While the notion of the Grim Reaper still being in town lurked at the back of my mind, he hadn't reacted when Xavier had verbally shared the Reapers' secrets with me. Maybe he'd react to a trick as overt as ferrying me as a passenger through the shadows. "Okay, I'll come."

Xavier took my hand and stepped into the shadows. Instant darkness closed in around us, claustrophobic and ice-cold, before fading back and revealing a corridor carpeted in blue and panelled in white. My head spun with vertigo when we set foot on solid ground again and the shadows faded, leaving only the hospital's corridor behind.

"They removed the police tape since I was last here," he said in an undertone. "I guess there was no proof it was murder, but we need to find out if Nero the Wonder and his friends came here recently."

"Might have to ask. It'll be quicker."

Xavier took us through the shadows again and landed

in the reception area, where the blue-haired witch behind the desk startled at the sight of us. "Sorry, didn't see you there. Can I help you?"

"Hey," I said. "I hope you don't mind my asking, but have you seen Nero the Wonder around lately? He has bright-pink hair, so it's hard to miss him."

Her jaw twitched. "Oh, him. Still causing trouble, is he?"

"Did he come to the hospital?" I asked. "In the past day, I mean?"

"I had to chase him and some of his hangers-on from filming a *video* in the corridor." Her nostrils flared. "They said the lighting was just right, but I can't believe they'd have the audacity. A man died here not two days ago."

"One of Nero's followers also dropped dead a few minutes ago," I admitted. "We believe she might have picked up the curse from the last victim."

"Oh." She took a step backwards. "Oh no. It *is* a curse? I hoped they had it wrong."

"It looks that way," said Xavier. "Unfortunately, the curse is likely to be spreading via a physical object, so it's vitally important that we find out whether Nero's followers might have touched anything that the last victim came into contact with."

She blinked. "I didn't think to look closely, but I saw them passing a book between them on the way out. I was inclined to ask if they stole it, but frankly, I was too glad to be rid of them to pursue the matter."

A book. "Thanks for telling us. We'd better get back to the library."

Xavier and I left. Not through the shadows, because the woman behind the desk looked freaked out enough already, and besides, I was still dizzy from our first trip. Instead, we walked through the automatic glass doors, which slid closed behind us.

"Why would they steal a book?" I asked. "Were they trying to figure out the curse themselves?"

"Edwin might be able to get the details out of them during their questioning." He came to a stop. "Ready to jump through the shadows again?"

Not really. "Sure. Guess your boss really isn't watching us."

"Did you think otherwise?" His brow furrowed, but he beckoned me into the shadows. When we stepped through and emerged into the library, we found it as chaotic as before.

Nero the Wonder and his entourage remained in the Reading Corner while the security trolls guarded a classroom door which I guessed that Edwin had picked out to use to question each suspect one at a time. It was, unfortunately, not the first time he'd had to use the library for this purpose nor the first occasion where we'd had to round up murder suspects in the Reading Corner.

I sought out Aunt Adelaide. "Can I talk to you for a second? Alone?"

"What is it, Rory?" She walked alongside me through the stacks of the research section and away from the gathering suspects.

I lowered my voice. "Nero's friends have one of our books."

"Which book?"

"One you loaned the staff at the hospital," I said. "I'm not sure which it was, but Xavier and I just spoke to the receptionist at the hospital, and she said Nero and his friends came in to film a video and left with one of our books."

"Why on earth would they take one of our textbooks?" she asked. "To read up on curses?"

"I don't know, but... have the police searched their possessions yet?"

"Not yet," said Estelle, overhearing us. "Don't worry, they know anything they touch might be cursed, and they're taking precautions. Why would Nero's friends take one of our books, though?"

"They got it from the hospital," I said in an undertone. "You don't think it might be how the curse was passed around?"

"That can't be possible," Aunt Adelaide said. "I handled all the books myself, and so did the rest of the staff. They can't be cursed."

Unless Nero or one of the others had cursed the book when they'd had it in their possession, of course, but that didn't account for the doctor's death. And why would Nero kill one of his own fans?

Estelle blew out a breath. "Anyone want to volunteer to speak to Mr Bennet again? If we find the book, the quickest way to find out if it's cursed or not is to take it to him."

"True," said Aunt Adelaide. "I hope it's *not* our book which carries the curse. There's still the question of how the first victim was cursed too. All the books were here at the time."

Except for the one which had been with the professor, but both of us had handled the book, and so had his assistant. If it was cursed, we'd know by now, right?

The classroom door behind the Reading Corner

opened, and one of the members of Nero the Wonder's entourage exited the room. When Edwin came to call in the next person, both Estelle and I went to waylay him.

The elf put on a long-suffering expression at the sight of us. "At this rate, I might have to move my office to your classroom."

I grimaced. "I shouldn't have let them into the library to begin with given how rude they were at the poetry night the other day."

"They're being perfectly polite to me," Edwin said. "Half of them barely know what a curse is. What did you want to ask, Aurora?"

"Did you confiscate anything from them?" I asked. "We just found out one of them has a book that belongs to the library. They stole it from the hospital."

"Is that so?" he said. "In that case, you can take it back once we release their personal possessions."

"There's a chance the book might have a curse on it, though," I said. "Yes, I know it's ironic that a book of curses might have ended up cursed..."

"Again?" said Edwin. "I seem to remember a similar incident a few months ago."

"He has a point," said Estelle in an undertone. "Maybe we should figure out how to curse-proof our books."

"We need to get that book away from anyone who might touch it." I gave Edwin a pleading look. "I promise I'll return the book if it turns out not to be cursed. We'll take it to Mr Bennet right away."

"Have you touched the book yourself?" he asked.

"Not since we loaned it out to the hospital," I said. "I don't think it was cursed then, which explains how the doctors were able to pass it among themselves without any issues, but it's the one connecting factor between the last two victims."

"Fine," he said. "The bags I confiscated are behind the back row of shelves in the Reading Corner. Do try not to get cursed, Aurora."

"Thanks." I left the classroom and dug in my pockets to find my winter gloves, slipping them on before heading over to the small pile of bags that had been confiscated from Nero the Wonder and his entourage. Aside from some expensive-looking video equipment, they carried little of import, but I did find the book lying at the bottom of someone's rucksack.

Sure enough, the book was the very same one I'd taken from Professor Colt. I drew in a deep breath as I picked it up, but nothing happened. I didn't particularly want to drop dead, though knowing Xavier would be the one to collect my soul made the prospect less scary than it might have seemed. Not that I wanted to tempt fate, either. I returned to the Reading Corner and held up the book for everyone to see. "Who was carrying this?"

Nobody answered, but Edwin stepped out of the classroom. "The quicker one of you confesses, the quicker you'll be able to go home. I'll take over from here."

I gave a quick scan of their faces to see if any of them showed signs of guilt, but most of them looked confused. Except for Nero the Wonder, but he'd gone oddly quiet, staring dejectedly at the spot where Nera had dropped dead.

With the book in hand, I prepared to take it to the curse-breaker, hoping that he wouldn't be as unhelpful as he'd been during our last conversation.

9

Xavier and I walked out of the library and crossed the square to the seafront. Not only did he insist on accompanying me to see Mr Bennet, but he also insisted on carrying the book himself. I'd lost *that* argument in approximately five seconds despite pointing out that I'd already touched the book while wearing gloves.

"How do you know the curse isn't going to harm you?" I held the book out of his reach. "I know you're a Reaper, but you should think about wearing gloves just in case."

"I don't have any, and if Reapers could drop dead from touching a simple cursed object, we wouldn't be much good at our jobs."

"The curse isn't a simple one, though," I argued. "Yes, I know you're undead, but really…"

Xavier's hand skimmed my shoulder as he reached for my arm, his fingers snagging the edge of the book. He was much taller than I was, so it was a losing battle on my part.

"You remember when I walked into the ocean and survived, don't you?" His breath tickled my neck, as cold as the breeze. "I won't let you be the one to take the risk."

I relented and dropped the book into his waiting hand. "Fine."

And that was that. We walked the rest of the way to the seafront and entered the curse-breaker's small shop, while Mr Bennet gave us another scowl from behind the counter.

"What is it this time?" he asked.

"I believe this book has a deadly curse on it." I indicated the book, which Xavier held up so that Mr Bennet could see the cover. "Xavier is carrying it because he's immune, but we think this is the source of a curse which has killed two people so far."

Mr Bennet looked stonily at me. "Get out."

"What?" I didn't move, but my shoulders tensed when he rose to his feet. "You don't have to touch it with your bare hands."

"I refuse to let you bring anything that's potentially deadly into my shop."

"You're a curse-breaker," I pointed out. "That's what you do, isn't it?"

"Foolish girl," he said. "I wouldn't be able to break a curse if I dropped dead the instant I touched it, would I?"

"I'm sure you can break the curse without touching the book," I said. "Can't you?"

"You can never be careful enough when it comes to experimental curses."

"So you admit the curse was definitely an experimental creation." He'd stubbornly refused to give us any useful information before, but two more people were dead, so it grated on my nerves to see him still digging his heels in. "Created by whom?"

The professor came to mind, but it left the question of *why* he would put a curse on someone. His interest in magical theory didn't necessarily translate to him wanting to use it in practise, and besides, if the book had been in his hands at the time, how had the first victim met his end?

"How did your family manage to get a curse put on one of their books, anyway?" Mr Bennet asked. "I assumed they were usually more careful with their property."

"They loaned the book to the hospital so the staff could use it to figure out what killed the wizard, Rufus," I explained. "I can only assume it was cursed at the hospital, because both people who've handled it since have dropped dead."

"And you brought it here," he said. "Have you touched it with your bare hands at all?"

"Yes, but before it was cursed," I said. "I don't expect you to be able to track the culprit, but I would appreciate it if you could break the curse on the book. Of course my aunt would pay your full rates."

"Naturally," he said. "Put it on the desk, and I'll run a couple of tests."

He took a hasty step back as Xavier lifted the book gingerly and placed it down on the wooden surface. Then he pulled out his wand and waved it in swirling patterns above the book while Xavier and I watched.

After several silent minutes, Mr Bennet put his wand away. "Thanks for wasting my time."

I blinked. "What do you mean?"

He grabbed the book and threw it at me. Despite my surprise, I managed to snag it by my fingertips before it fell to the ground. "Wait, it's not cursed?"

"No, it is not," he said. "It's not the first time your aunt has made completely the wrong guess, is it?"

"It was my guess," I told him. "Besides, it's the only clue we had, since the sole person who witnessed the first victim's death was the Grim Reaper, and he refused to share that information with anyone except for you."

"She's right," said Xavier. "You told us that you spoke to my boss but not what he shared with you. If you hadn't kept that information to yourself, we might have been able to prevent the other two deaths. Which object was the curse placed on the first time around?"

Mr Bennet's lip curled. "If your boss refused to share any information with you, I assume he had his reasons. No doubt he suspected you'd manage to get more people killed."

"You're blaming *me* for their deaths?" Xavier's voice was quiet, shocked.

"No," said the curse-breaker. "The fault lies with your girlfriend, who is no doubt the one who insisted on dragging you here on a false alarm."

"False alarm?" I echoed. "The curse seems pretty real to me, considering someone just dropped dead in the library."

"Don't play smart with me, Aurora," he said. "If you must know, the first body was decontaminated at the scene. You don't think that boss of yours wouldn't have recognised that kind of curse?"

I stared at him. "You mean to say the Grim Reaper decontaminated the body? He removed the curse?"

"You heard me."

So the Grim Reaper *had* stopped the curse, but the killer had struck again, and the curse had started anew. Did that mean the killer knew the Grim Reaper was no longer around? As for Xavier's boss, if he'd thought the curse had been dealt with, then what reason did he have for leaving town? If he was genuinely trying to test his apprentice, he had a terrible sense of timing, but if anything, this further proved he wasn't hiding nearby and watching us. If he'd been within reach, he'd have surely acted to remove the curse as he had with the first body.

"Does the Grim Reaper know *who* put the curse on Rufus?" I asked.

"If he did, he didn't enlighten me," said Mr Bennet. "Now, will you stop badgering me and leave?"

Fine. I kept a tight grip on the book as I left the shop with Xavier at my heels. "I can't believe him."

"Who, Mr Bennet or my boss?" Xavier spoke in a quiet voice which contained a hint of shock. "He removed the curse from Rufus himself. I feel like I ought to have known given his behaviour when we arrived at the scene of his death."

"Why did he leave town, then?" I asked. "That's what I don't get. You've searched the town on foot enough times that you'd have run into him by now if he stuck around, but you'd think he'd have suspected the killer might try again."

"Exactly," he said. "Something doesn't add up."

"No kidding," I said. "Was he that confident the killer wouldn't strike again?"

The killer, meanwhile, remained at large, and even

Nero the Wonder and his friends being in custody didn't guarantee the rest of us were safe.

In the meantime, Xavier and I returned to the library, where I sought out Aunt Adelaide. To my surprise, the Reading Corner had been vacated, though Nero and his friends had left the chairs and beanbags in disarray.

"Rory." Aunt Adelaide strode over to us. "Don't tell me Mr Bennet refused to help again. He didn't, did he?"

"He said the curse isn't on the book." I fished in my bag for the book. "Did Edwin finish questioning Nero and his friends?"

"Edwin took the few people he wanted to question further to the police station," she said. "Unfortunately, since one of them was Nero himself, everyone else went with him."

"Figures," I said. "Does he have a short list of suspects?"

"A very short one," she replied. "The trolls took everything they confiscated from the suspects."

"Without touching anything, I hope," I said. "Given that the book didn't turn out to be cursed after all."

Her brow furrowed. "All three victims came into contact with the same object?"

"I don't think so, since the Grim Reaper decontaminated the first body," I said. "According to Mr Bennet, anyway."

"The Grim Reaper?" she echoed.

"Yes." Xavier's carefully neutral tone renewed my annoyance at his wayward boss. "Mr Bennet relented and told me of their discussion after he found Rufus's body."

"Unfortunately, it seems the killer then opted to use the same method again." I removed the textbook from my bag and offered it to Aunt Adelaide, who took it from me.

"Which means only the most recent two victims came into contact with the same object."

"Let's see what we have here." She flipped open the book I'd given her. "This one came from the university, didn't it? I may have to give it back to the hospital staff."

"Why'd Nero's friends steal it, I wonder?" Nobody had actually owned up to taking the book, in fact. "Did Edwin find out?"

"Not that I'm aware of," said Aunt Adelaide. "The one certainty is that the curse has yet to pass on to anyone else —or it hadn't before they left the library, anyway."

"Is that bad news?" Sylvester swooped down to land on a nearby shelf. "Should one of us fix that?"

"Honestly, Sylvester." Aunt Adelaide shook her head at the owl. "Estelle is at the police station, too, Rory. She went there as soon as she finished talking to that girl from the university. I forget her name."

"Who, Lara?" I hadn't even known she'd stuck around after the police had shown up. "She works for Professor Colt as his assistant. I think she wanted to ask Estelle about her thesis."

Professor Colt had also had access to the book on curses… but we'd established the book wasn't cursed after all. Yes, the university was certainly a likely place for developing experimental magic, but there seemed no reason whatsoever to unleash a deadly curse on unwitting victims without any motive.

"Estelle wasn't thrilled to leave her essay, but she wanted to go with Edwin," said Aunt Adelaide. "Most likely to stop Candace from volunteering instead."

Sylvester scoffed. "If you ask me, Candace knows better than any of you how to ask the right questions."

Was he implying she'd consulted the Book of Questions? Unlikely. Except for her brief appearance when Nera's body had shown up, she'd displayed zero interest in finding out the cause of the curse, and I'd never known her to rely on the Forbidden Room either. I assumed she was well aware that it would usually avoid giving her a straight answer, and she consequently preferred to rely on her own research materials instead.

In any case, I ignored the owl and turned back to Aunt Adelaide. "I think I should let Edwin know. I'm not sure even his troll guards can handle the entirety of Nero the Wonder's entourage at once, to be honest."

"You want to go to the police station?" Xavier asked. "I'll go with you, then. Since I'm immune to the curse, I might be able to help search the bags they confiscated from Nero's followers."

"That's a good idea," said Aunt Adelaide. "I'll finish cleaning up this mess."

Xavier was uncharacteristically quiet as we walked towards the seafront again, but I didn't blame him. His boss had disappeared not to solve a murder but because he placed so little value on telling the truth even to his own apprentice that he'd seen fit to abandon him in a time when we could really have used his help. Admittedly, he might have had another reason for taking off, but not letting Xavier know he was leaving was unfair to say the least.

We found the police station in a predictable state of disarray, with Nero the Wonder's followers complaining at anyone who would listen about the unfair treatment of their idol. It took me a while to spot Estelle pressed against the back wall behind one of the security trolls.

Relief crossed her expression when she spotted us approaching her.

"Hey." Estelle squeezed out from behind the troll to join Xavier and me. "Did my mum send you to rescue me?"

"What in the world is going on in here?" I asked.

"Nobody will let Edwin question Nero," she said. "They're bleating about his innocence without listening to any of the charges. It's a nightmare."

"Can't the trolls keep them out?" Xavier said.

"They're scared of touching anyone in case they run into the curse." Estelle rolled her eyes. "Did you manage to fix the book?"

"The curse turned out not to be on the book after all."

Estelle swore under her breath. "Then where is it?"

"Mr Bennet still thinks the curse is on an object," I said. "Has anyone figured out what Nera had on her when she died?"

"No," she said. "Ah—Edwin, have you got everyone's possessions in here?"

The elf policeman shuffled along the back wall towards us. "Aurora, have you broken the curse?"

"We spoke to Mr Bennet, and he said the curse wasn't on the book we thought it was," I said. "Where're the suspects' other possessions?"

"I had to ask one of my wizards on the staff team to transport everyone's possessions into a spare room." He ducked under a flailing arm as the nearest troll kept one of Nero's pink-haired followers from getting near us. "I'd rather not keep a cursed object on the property, though."

"I know, but it's better than letting it run amok among the public," I said. "Who was carrying the book, anyway?"

"You can't arrest him!" bellowed the red-haired wizard I'd seen earlier. "You can't lock up Nero the Wonder!"

Nero himself hovered near the interrogation room, making an appeal to a security troll, while his fans milled around him.

Edwin cleared his throat. "Nobody is getting locked up, but if you want to go home in a reasonable time, then I'd suggest you stop getting under my trolls' feet. Can those of you who've already been cleared please wait outside?"

"We can't leave him," said the wizard. "We're his fan club."

"I'm sure he's brave enough to submit to a questioning without your help," Estelle said. "Nero, you'd rather everyone waited outside, wouldn't you?"

Nero's expression showed bewilderment when she addressed him. "They wanna support me, you get me?"

"All Edwin wants to do is talk to the people who directly saw and interacted with Nera right before and after her death," Estelle continued, pushing her advantage now that she had their attention. "We don't believe any of you meant to hurt Nera, but to figure out how she died, we need to find out what she was doing at the time."

"Exactly," said Edwin. "Kindly please stop hassling my guards so I can ask Nero a few questions."

That seemed to mollify them, but they remained in the lobby, trying to look behind every closed door and generally being a nuisance. Xavier, Estelle, and I made our way through to the interrogation room before Edwin closed the door.

Inside, Nero the Wonder sat on a chair in his usual

casual manner, his bright-pink hair in disarray and a mildly annoyed look on his face.

"You're ruining the vibe," he told the elf policeman. "I'm supposed to be filming a video, not being treated like a criminal."

"I'm the chief of police in this town," said Edwin. "If you truly want to buy a seafront property in Ivory Beach, then you're going to have to answer my questions."

"Fine." He slumped back. "Fire away."

"Did you know Nera was cursed?"

"Cursed?" he exclaimed. "No, that's impossible."

"It's possible." I felt the slightest guilty twinge at Edwin's exasperated look, but I pressed on. "Did you go to the hospital to film a video?"

He frowned. "What does that have to do with anything?"

"We found a book from the library in one of your bags," I said. "A book we loaned to the hospital staff."

"What?" he said. "I thought you were looking for a murderer, not the thief."

"Did you see the body of the other victim?" Estelle asked. "Is that where you got the book?"

"I didn't get the book." He looked at Estelle as if he thought she had a screw loose. "I didn't take it."

"Did Nera?"

"I dunno. She's dead."

"We won't let them take you!" A hammering noise came from the door, which crashed open a moment later. Nero's entourage poured in, led by a wizard with a large tattoo of Nero the Wonder's face on his forearms, complete with neon-pink hair.

"I told you to wait outside," Edwin said.

"We won't let you arrest him!" said the wizard. "We'll go to jail instead, gladly."

Honestly. "All we want to know is which of you saw the body of the doctor who died at the hospital."

"Why'd you want to know that?" Nero said.

"Because the curse somehow spread to Nera that way." Not that anyone else was listening.

"Ah." Nero shifted in his seat. "Well, I *saw* the body, but I didn't touch it or anything else."

"Then who took the book?" Estelle raised her voice, but nobody paid her the slightest bit of attention. It also struck me that Xavier had disappeared, but if he'd used his shadow trick to sneak out, I didn't blame him a bit.

Edwin gave us all a pleading look. "I can't work with this."

"Try asking the curse-breaker," I suggested. "I don't think we're going to be much help here, though."

Estelle and I left Nero's followers to their lament and returned to the lobby, where we found Xavier waiting for us.

"Sorry I left you in there," he said. "I imagined taking you through the shadows would invite unwelcome questions."

"Honestly, I don't think any of them were paying much attention." Meanwhile, poor Edwin couldn't get a word in edgeways.

But did their slavish devotion to their hero extend to helping him cover up two murders?

10

"What a nightmare," said Estelle as the three of us left the police station. "I hope Edwin and the others are careful."

"No kidding." If one of the others came into contact with the curse before we'd managed to identify it, then it might lead to more needless deaths, but preventing any of Nero the Wonder's entourage from following him around seemed a futile endeavour even for Edwin's security trolls.

"I'll go back later to help sort through the confiscated items," said Xavier. "Maybe by then, someone will have confessed to taking the library book."

"Yeah, it's a weird choice if they weren't interested in the curse," I said. "The book might not have any definite information pointing to the culprit, but it might be worth speaking to the last person who borrowed it from the library again."

"Who, the professor?" Xavier said. "I suppose it can't hurt at this stage if there isn't anyone else to ask."

"There's always the Book of Questions," said Estelle. "Though it's not known for being reliable in its answers."

"Exactly." I had yet to come up with a precise question that wouldn't lead to Sylvester slithering out of answering. "Should I head up to campus and talk to the professor? I'll come straight back to the library afterwards."

"Of course," said Estelle. "The library's closed for the rest of the day unless my mum says otherwise."

"Then I'll go with Rory." Xavier was still notably more subdued than usual after the curse-breaker's unwelcome revelation about his boss.

We parted ways with Estelle in the town square, Xavier and I continuing up the high street and towards the university campus. On the way, we passed the vampires' church, closed for the day with its windows shuttered and its spires dark against the pale-grey sky.

"I wonder what I'd have to promise Evangeline in exchange for her help solving the murders," I remarked. "Laney's immortal soul and my dad's journal, probably."

"I wouldn't ask her anything," Xavier said. "Not even where to find my boss."

"Evangeline does know where he is, though," I pointed out. "I'm starting to wish we'd asked her when she showed up at your house, to be honest."

"I refuse to beg her for answers." His sharp tone took me by surprise, but his voice softened a moment later. "I'm not angry with you, Rory, but I wish I knew what my boss was playing at."

"I know." I slid my hand into his and gave a reassuring squeeze, trying to mask my annoyance at the Grim Reaper for toying with his mild-mannered apprentice until he'd lost his temper. He'd better have a bloody good reason for vanishing, that was for sure.

When we reached the campus, we retraced our steps to the building where Professor Colt worked. Once again, Xavier opted to wait in the corridor outside while I knocked on the professor's office door.

"Come in!" He looked up at me. "You again? Did I forget to return another book?"

"No," I said. "I wanted to ask you a couple of questions about curses, if that's okay?"

"Of course." He waved a hand to invite me into the office. "Ask me anything."

I closed the door behind me. "This is going to sound like a weird question, but if you knew you were in the company of a cursed object, would you be able to use some kind of tracking spell to pin down which object the curse was on? Like the magical equivalent of a metal detector?"

"That's a tricky one," he said. "It's certainly possible to track down something magical, but there isn't a way to distinguish between a cursed object and a regular magical artefact. Not without getting your hands on the object in question, at any rate, and it'd take a curse-breaker's finesse to narrow it down."

Typical. If Mr Bennet refused point-blank to get within sniffing distance of the curse, then Edwin would doubtless have trouble convincing him to nose through all the suspects' confiscated possessions in the hope of pinning down the curse.

"There *is* a magical tracking spell, though?" I asked.

"There's a spell for almost anything," he responded. "Curses might be tricky and hard to pin down, but they ultimately work the same as any other spell at a basic level."

That made sense. The textbook definition of curses was 'hostile spells directed at a person', so it made sense that it would be hard to distinguish a cursed object from something relatively mundane in the magical world without getting close enough to risk touching the object yourself.

Except there was one aspect which distinguished this particular curse from the textbook definition. "Can one cursed object affect multiple people if they all handled it unknowingly? I mean, it doesn't have to be directed at a particular target, does it?"

"Theoretically, yes." A shadow fell over his expression. "A strong enough curse can reach unlimited targets. That's why there are such strong penalties attached to them and heavy fines for those who are found to have such an item in their possession. I remember there was once a notorious cursed mask which caused anyone who handled it to lose their fingers. You can imagine the chaos that wreaked before the magical authorities managed to safely contain it."

A shudder ran through me. "Is a curse always transferred by touching the object with one's bare hands, then?"

"That's the simplest way," he said. "The target must have direct contact with the curse in some manner. There are exceptions, though, like items of clothing which start to strangle anyone who puts them on or books which curse anyone who reads them."

Hmm. Was that where we'd gone wrong with the cursed book? Mr Bennet had insisted it wasn't cursed, but

Edwin had reminded me that we'd faced a similar dilemma the week I'd moved into the library in which a curse turned out to have been put on a piece of paper hidden among a book's pages. The curse had consequently escaped detection, but I hadn't found any scraps of paper inside the textbook, and given how it'd been passed around, it would likely have fallen out by now.

"How long does a curse usually take to come into effect, then?" I asked.

"That varies too," he said. "Even following a set of instructions. With experimental curses, the effect might take weeks or months to activate."

That couldn't be the case this time around, given how close together the two deaths had taken place, which pointed to the likelihood of the killer having planted their cursed object on the victim at the hospital before Nera had stolen it from his body. Question was, what had they intended to achieve? Their choice of victims remained as confusing as ever. Unless it'd all been some kind of stunt by Nero the Wonder to gain publicity, but that didn't strike me as quite right either.

"Speaking of experimental curses," I said. "If they're illegal, then how are you able to research them? I mean, do the magical authorities keep tabs on you?"

"The university's rules strictly prohibit *using* illegal curses, of course," said the professor. "Research isn't prohibited, but they do insist on inspections every few months to make sure none of us is hiding any cursed objects on the property. Rather unnecessary, in my opinion, but I suppose all magic carries its own risks. It's just as likely that a potions expert might poison a rival or something similar."

Fair point. I might have had a mostly negative experience with curses, but all magic had its uses, and having an interest in curses didn't necessarily mean one would employ them against others. Besides, I couldn't think why a reclusive professor would unleash a lethal curse on a bunch of strangers.

"So they'd notice if someone was developing a deadly curse and actually putting it into practise, then?" I asked.

"Of course they would," he said. "There's certainly been incidents of that nature, here and elsewhere, but most are reluctant to discuss them for good reason. I'd suggest consulting that wonderful library of yours if you'd like to know more."

"I will," I said. "Thanks for the help."

I had an inkling that information would be locked away in the high-security sections I wasn't yet qualified to go into, but Estelle and Aunt Adelaide had full access to the library, and they'd also remember if any illegal curses had run amok on the campus over the last few decades. In any case, I suspected I'd hit a wall with the professor. He seemed entirely oblivious to the world outside of his office.

I left the building with Xavier, my mind ticking over the new details on curses I'd unearthed. Until we found out which object the curse had been put on, though, tracing the person responsible would be all but impossible. Either Edwin convinced Mr Bennet to help, or we'd be left in limbo until the only other person who might know the culprit returned from his inconvenient absence. Not that Xavier seemed confident of the latter. He remained in a taciturn silence as we walked, slowing his pace as we neared the library.

"What do you want to do now?" I asked. "I know the library's closed, but I should help clean up the mess Nero and his friends left in the Reading Corner."

"I ought to head back to the police station," said Xavier.

"Seriously?" My brows shot up. "It's up to you, but I doubt they've calmed down in the last half hour."

"No, but I can handle cursed objects without being affected," he said. "I have my doubts that Mr Bennet will be willing to volunteer, and this is the quickest way to find the cause."

"If you're sure."

"If my boss was here, he'd tell me not to do it." A flinty expression entered his eyes. "But he's not, so he'll have to deal with the consequences."

My heart fluttered uneasily. "Xavier…"

"I'm fine." He pulled me into a hug. "I'll see you later, okay?"

"Sure." I squeezed him back. "Don't let him get to you."

"I won't." He released me and glided away while I hovered on the doorstep for a moment, a significant part of me wanting to hurry after him.

There wasn't much I could do to help, either with searching for the curse or with finding his elusive boss, so I re-entered the library. To my surprise, Estelle had almost finished cleaning up the Reading Corner.

"I needed a break from my thesis," she said. "Besides, I wanted to make sure Nero's friends didn't swipe any of the books, and my mum took Sylvester with her to search the high-security rooms."

"She did?" Did that mean she thought she might find

something useful in the part of the library which wasn't open to the public?

"Yeah, a few minutes ago," she said. "How was campus?"

"I spoke to the professor again," I said. "Didn't learn much, though, except that the magical community tends to keep incidents with runaway curses under wraps. Has anything similar ever happened on campus before?"

Her brow wrinkled. "Not that I'm aware of, but my mum will know. I think she'd have already brought it up if she knew of an occasion where a runaway curse was causing people to drop dead, though."

"True." I accompanied her to the front desk, noting that the Book of Questions lay on top of the record book. The book's cover was black leather with no title on it, but no other volume looked quite as distinct. "Were you going to check the Forbidden Room?"

"Thought I might," she said. "I *can* technically go with my mum into the high-security rooms, but I'm sceptical as to whether they'll find anything in there. It seems like the killer created this curse on their own."

"Without any help?" My mind drifted back to the professor. "Or by following instructions which nobody else had access to?"

"Most likely the latter," she said. "Yes, the top-security sections of the library *do* contain books with instructions for creating curses which are illegal in practise, but to my knowledge, none of them has been removed from the library in years."

"I'm surprised you're allowed to keep them," I remarked.

"Oh, the magical authorities don't always *like* it, but

we're the only location in the region with sufficient security spells to store dangerous books," she said. "They're forever badgering us for paperwork, of course, but we have proof that we keep those books from being viewed by the public."

My gaze went to the Book of Questions. "Do you think the Book might be able to tell you where the curse is located? Xavier is checking everything Edwin confiscated from Nero and his friends, but since he's a Reaper, he can't be affected by the curse."

She picked up the large leather-bound book with the silver question mark on the spine. "This is a long shot, but it's worth a try."

"Go ahead," I said. "I'll try to think of a good question before it's my turn."

"All right." Estelle opened the book. "I wish to enter the Forbidden Room."

A faint roaring sounded, like wind whistling, and Estelle vanished into its pages. The book toppled back onto the desk while I headed towards the family's living quarters.

With the rest of the day free, I finally had an opportunity to work on my dad's journal, but my focus was utterly spent. I got out the translator document and sat on the sofa, but I found myself pacing in circles instead.

Get a grip, Rory. I'd just sat down again when the soft sound of footsteps came from the stairs. Laney must be awake. I was surprised the ruckus hadn't disturbed her sooner.

Sure enough, Laney poked her head into the living room. "It's quiet in here. Has everyone taken off?"

"We temporarily closed the library for the day," I said. "Did you hear about the death—?"

"Rory, I might sleep like the undead, but I also have sensitive hearing," she said. "The curse has spread to Nero the Wonder and his friends, right?"

"One of his followers died, but we have no idea which object the curse is actually on," I said. "Estelle is asking the Book of Questions, and Aunt Adelaide is checking the library's high-security rooms, but there's not much else we can do."

Her gaze went to the journal lying on the sofa. "You have the day free to work on that, then."

"In theory." I rubbed my forehead. "But I can't concentrate, and there's too much else on my mind."

"I get that," she said. "Not other people's thoughts, though. My own are enough, thanks."

"Is Evangeline bothering you?"

"No more than usual," she said. "Everything has to be a mind game with the vampires, though. It gets kind of exhausting after a while."

"Yeah, I can imagine," I said. "Did she drop any more hints about our missing Reaper?"

"You still haven't found him?"

"Nope," I said. "Xavier is ticked off, and I don't blame him. I wondered if Evangeline might have dropped any hints."

"None whatsoever, but the other vamps don't often discuss the Reapers," she said. "Not because they're afraid of them, more disinterested. Evangeline is the one who likes to pay visits to the Grim Reaper."

"I'm guessing their rivalry is because she thinks there can only be one cranky, all-powerful immortal in town." I rolled my eyes. "Or she's concerned he might reap her soul. Anyway, I can't imagine what they spend their time chatting about."

"You?"

"*Me?*" I frowned. "You think the Grim Reaper uses her as a confidant to share his annoyance that his apprentice is dating a mortal?"

Laney snorted. "You never know. Maybe he's secretly setting Xavier up with someone else."

"Nah, Reapers aren't allowed relationships," I said. "They're not allowed to get married, even to each other, and they can't have kids. Side effect of being technically dead."

Her eyes bulged. "Seriously? So you and Xavier—"

I had abrupt regrets about bringing up the subject. "Our plan is to continue to see one another for as long as we can. It's a miracle we got that much from His Grumpiness."

Laney frowned. "That's ridiculous. I mean, vamps can't have children either, but they can get married and otherwise make their own decisions regarding their romantic lives."

"Reapers are supposed to be impartial." I scooped up the journal, absently turning the pages. "They're supposed to be removed from humanity as a whole, because otherwise it puts their jobs at risk. I imagine it causes headaches for the council if their Reapers start trying to spare the lives of their loved ones or begging for exemptions."

"There's a difference between asking to save someone's soul when the time comes and being in love with someone."

Her words struck my chest like an arrow. *Was* I in love with Xavier? I couldn't deny the tugging in my chest every time I thought of him, even when he wasn't around, nor the fact that even imagining him disappearing from my life was inconceivable. But did he feel the same for me?

I blinked hard. "Whatever Xavier feels, if the Grim Reaper *doesn't* come back, he's next in line as his replacement. No denying that. Anyway, how are your lessons going?"

"Good," she said, thankfully seizing on the change of subject. "I'm learning to keep my instincts reined in, and I'm starting to work on feigning being human well enough to fool the average person. It's not impossible for vamps to blend in even among normals, so it must be doable."

Oh. She probably wanted to visit her family. A jolt of guilt hit me at the reminder of the life she'd been severed from when she'd come to live here. She'd insisted she preferred the magical world, but she'd had to leave almost everything behind. Even being turned into a vampire hadn't erased that.

"That's good." I skipped back through the journal's pages to find my former place. "With vamps throwing parties in the normal world, they must be used to blending in."

"Speaking of vampires." Her gaze followed my hands as they turned the pages of the journal. "I probably shouldn't ask questions about that, huh."

I hesitated for an instant. I'd be lying if I said part of me didn't worry about Evangeline reading the journal's contents from her mind, since there was no doubt that Evangeline *was* trying to mine her for information. On the other hand, she gained at least a portion of her knowledge through guesswork. Look at how she'd correctly deduced the Grim Reaper's absence. Besides, I was sick of keeping a barrier up between me and my best friend.

The moment I read the truth from the journal's pages, Evangeline would find out, but weeks of delaying hadn't quenched my desire to know. And I wanted to let Laney in on it too.

I found the right page and settled back in my seat. "Nah, ask all the questions you like. I think I might be able to focus more if someone else is here."

Her brows shot up. "Even though I spend every other evening with your immortal enemy?"

"Evangeline isn't my enemy. She's just untrustworthy. But I'm also dating the Reaper, so…"

A grin appeared on her mouth. "I like how you think."

"It's not like I've found anything incriminating so far," I added. "Though it's taking a while to get through, because my dad had this habit of annotating his entries at a later date and confusing the translator spell. When I left off, though, he'd gone on this trip to Europe in search of a rare book."

"A magical one?"

"I imagine it was," I said. "It sounds like the village where it was located was hidden by magical wards. Also, a group of vampires showed up at the inn where he was staying, looking for the same location."

"So that's how he and the vamps started butting heads?"

"I bet it is," I said. "He was hiding his own magical status from the normals at the time too. Didn't even have his wand."

"Risky, that."

"I know." I moved the translated document alongside the journal and continued to read, while Laney sat and occasionally offered a comment. I'd already filled her in on my dad's history with the library and how he'd left to marry my mum and have me, but the more of his journal I read, the more I began to suspect that his hunt for rare books had given him a connection to his old life. No wonder he hadn't been able to resist.

I finally did it, read the next entry. I found a way into the village. The shielding spell was a complicated one, but the vampires were persistent enough to comb the entire forest, and I decided it would save time for me to follow them. Sure enough, I found a gap in the shielding spell and managed to slip through without being detected.

I have to say, it's very strange to experience magic as an outsider. It took a while to convince the townsfolk that I was indeed a wizard, albeit one without a wand. It doesn't help that my German is rusty. But they didn't throw me out, so I think I succeeded at winning them over. Now to find the book.

I raised a brow at Laney. "I think he got a kick out of the adventure aspect of the whole thing, to tell you the truth."

"The poor guy had been outside the magical world for years," she said. "He was stuck looking after a toddler, as well."

"Oi." I gave her a mock stern look. "I was perfectly well behaved, I'll have you know."

"Joking, joking," she said. "Seriously, though, he probably missed it all. It's a shame he couldn't have both."

I looked down at the journal, a familiar clenching sensation in my chest. Not for the first time, I wished the magical authorities had been less strict on the rules for inviting normals into their world. Growing up in the library would have been a different life altogether. I hadn't minded spending my childhood in the bookshop, of course, but that *what if* always lurked in the back of my mind.

Laney's hand brushed my knee. "I'm sorry, Rory. I shouldn't have reminded you."

I shook my head. "It's all right. I'm glad *you* got to experience this world, at least. Let's find out if the vampires found the shortcut into the magically hidden town."

I turned the page and read the translation. *I found the book's owner. He's an eccentric collector called Hermann Junior and he inherited the book from a great-great grandfather or something similar. He seemed loath to part with it, but he said he'd consider my price. It'd be easier if I were able to tell him about my history at the library, but I couldn't risk dragging Adelaide into this. She has young children, after all, and I can't help thinking of Rory at home...*

My eyes stung, but I kept reading. Then I came to a passage which made the blood freeze in my veins.

Something unusual has happened. I caught sight of a peculiar shadow following me around the village which vanished when I tried to get a closer look. I know the signs. There is a Reaper in the area.

"Rory?" Laney peered into my eyes. "What's wrong?"

I shivered. "Can't you read my thoughts?"

"I told you I have control over the ability, right?" she said. "I try to knock before being invited in. You don't have to tell me, anyway."

"It's okay," I said. "I'm pretty sure my dad met a Reaper

while he was nosing around the hidden village. Not sure which one, though."

It couldn't be *the* Grim Reaper, surely, but the description was similar enough to give me chills.

The Reaper finally showed his face tonight. It's the first time I've actually set eyes on one of them, since they aren't meant to show their faces in front of regular people. I have to admit it gave me a fright at first to see a shadow turn into a hooded figure carrying a scythe. Though that paled in comparison to his words. He told me outright that I should leave the village at once and abandon my attempts to procure the book. He said I was making a huge mistake in angering the vampires.

I put the book down, dread coursing through me. The Reaper had been trying to warn him off angering the vampires, and I had a horrible feeling my dad had discarded that advice.

He'd got his hands on the book anyway while the Founders had made him into their enemy. That much I knew, but I never would have guessed a *Reaper* would have tried to dissuade him. Whatever had happened to their rules about not interacting with mortals?

Were the Founders truly dangerous enough for the Reapers to consider breaking their rules?

11

Despite my multiplying misgivings, I read on. *Despite the Reaper's warnings, I had a meeting secured with the bookshop owner and I preferred not to abruptly cancel. The good news is that he was willing to hear me out and I successfully procured the book from him. I left the village in triumph, and I did not see the vampires. Strange of a Reaper to warn me, but I saw no signs of him when I left the inn.*

I put the journal down. "I think I need to take a breather."

"I don't blame you," Laney said. "That sounds pretty intense. Your dad was stalked by a Reaper?"

"Apparently," I said. "The vampires didn't catch him up for a while, I don't think. I was about three when all this was going on, and he didn't die until nearly two decades later."

"Rory..." she began.

"I'm good." I blinked a couple of times. "Honestly, I'm glad he did get to keep something of his connection to the magical world, even if he did insist on getting himself entangled with vampires and Reapers."

In fact, it said a lot for the Reapers' and the vampires' animosity that a Reaper had tried to warn my dad to avoid angering them. Didn't that count as breaking the rules? I'd have to ask Xavier.

Both of us startled when Cass walked into the living room, looking between us and the journal with a bewildered expression on her face. "What are you two doing?"

"I thought you'd guessed." Sometimes I forgot Cass *wasn't* the mind-reader out of the pair of them. "Wait, is Estelle around?"

"No, why?"

"She went to ask the Book of Questions something a while ago."

She ought to have come back by now, surely. I returned the journal to my bag while Cass and Laney glared at one another in one of their silent battles of wills.

"Don't start fighting, you two," I told them. "I'm going to see where Estelle's disappeared to."

I walked out into the library and headed for the desk. The Book of Questions lay on the desk, exactly where it'd been when Estelle had disappeared, but I hadn't heard her come back.

"Sylvester?" I called out, but the owl didn't reply. He must still be helping Aunt Adelaide search the library's high-security sections for information on curses. So why had Estelle not returned from the Forbidden Room yet? Unless she'd wandered elsewhere, but Laney's vampire hearing ought to have picked up on her footsteps.

I returned to the living room. "Laney, did you hear Estelle walking around while we were in here?"

"No, why?"

Cass rolled her eyes. "Calm down. Estelle doesn't need you panicking over her."

"I'm not panicking." Nevertheless, I returned to the desk and picked up the Book of Questions. I hadn't given my own question enough thought, but if Estelle had run into trouble, I needed to get her out of that room.

I flipped the book open to reveal its blank, yellowing pages. "I wish to enter the Forbidden Room."

At once, I toppled headfirst into oblivion, hands flailing, the book no longer in my grip. Then my feet slammed into the soft carpet of a small square room with black-painted walls covered in considerably more glitter than they had been during my previous visit. The room also contained a large cage which I'd never seen before. Estelle sat inside it with a resigned expression on her face, with Spark the pixie perched on her shoulder. How had he ended up stuck in here as well?

"Estelle?" I examined the cage, which had no door or obvious way to let her out.

My cousin blinked at me. "Rory, what are you doing in here?"

"Rescuing you, apparently." She didn't know Sylvester controlled the room, but if his secret ended up being exposed, it served him right for shutting her inside a cage. "Why did the room lock you up?"

"I have no idea," she said. "Spark followed me in here by accident. The instant I appeared in this room, the cage slammed down on us and wouldn't let us out."

Oh no. Sylvester hated the pixie, and the fact that Spark had covered the Forbidden Room in pink and purple sparkles would probably have sent the owl over the edge.

"Hey!" I addressed the room in general. "Let them out. Did you even answer any question?"

Nobody replied. I rotated on my heel, but aside from the cage, the room was empty.

"I asked my question," Estelle said. "Didn't work."

"How did Spark end up coming in here with you?" I asked. "Because that might be the problem, since only one person is meant to be in here at a time."

"I have no idea," she said. "He came to watch me when I opened the book, and I guess he got sucked in by accident."

"Then that's hardly your fault." Honestly. Sylvester could hear every word we said, I didn't doubt, as much as he enjoyed pretending otherwise. I might have tried to use magic to get her out of the cage, but I had the distinct impression Sylvester wouldn't have made it that easy for us.

I reached into my pocket for my Biblio-Witch Inventory and started by using a vanishing spell on the glitter, figuring it was best to start off by resolving the source of Sylvester's annoyance. The pink and purple sparkles disappeared. So magic did work in here, then.

Focusing my attention on the cage, I pressed my finger to the word *vanish*.

"I already tried that," said Estelle. "No spell can get rid of this cage, at least not one I've thought of yet."

"Weird," I said. "The Book usually kicks you out of the room when it can't answer your question."

The pixie made a chittering noise and beat its wings. Another thought occurred to me.

"Maybe the pixie needs to ask a question as well."

"You think?" Estelle spoke in the pixie's language while Spark made a similar series of noises before facing the room from behind the cage's bars.

After he'd finished speaking, the room began to spin in circles. Estelle yelped and grabbed the side of the cage for balance while Spark yelped as he was propelled from side to side in mid-air.

"What did he ask?" I caught the side of the cage to keep from falling into it while the room continued to spin.

"I don't know—" Estelle's words cut off as she and the pixie vanished.

Then the cage disappeared too. I tumbled back and landed on the wall—which was now the floor—my knees hitting the hard surface with a thud which made my teeth rattle in my skull. "Ow. What was that in aid of?"

No response came from the room. I lifted my head. "You didn't think Estelle had better things to do than argue with you for an hour? I thought you respected her need to work on her thesis."

"There is glitter everywhere." The owl's voice came out of the walls. "My room is ruined. Ruined!"

"I got rid of the glitter." I indicated the blank walls. "You're welcome. What did the pixie ask you?"

"Something inane."

"You were just screwing with them both, weren't you?" I pushed into a sitting position, wincing at the pain in my knees. "Sylvester, you know people are dying from an unknown curse, don't you? I take it Estelle didn't ask the right question?"

No answer came, but I already knew she hadn't. Nor had the pixie, apparently.

"Answer mine, then." A dozen possible questions came to mind, but instead, I found myself asking, "Where is the Grim Reaper? Wait, ignore that question. Who has the information on how to stop the curse and find the perpetrator?"

The room began to spin again. I hastened to brace myself against the wall, but the room flipped over again, sending me sprawling into another heap... inside a cage.

The owl's voice cut through my exasperated groan. "You should know better than to ask multiple questions in one go."

I sat up against the wall, my knees protesting. "Sylvester, this isn't a joke. If you can't answer my question, then at least let me out of the room."

He wouldn't know where the Grim Reaper was, since he could only respond accurately to questions whose answers lay in the library. For that reason, he'd only be able to point me in the direction of the killer if they'd been in the library themselves or had otherwise left evidence behind.

"One question only," said the owl's voice. "I told you."

"Look, if you keep me in here indefinitely, someone else is going to figure out you're the person controlling this room." I drew my knees up to my chest, a headache building. I'd respected the owl's privacy, mostly because I had little doubt he'd ban me from the Room altogether if I gave him away, but I was starting to think it wasn't worth the effort.

"Let me answer your first question, you impatient spatula," he said. "The answer lies with his enemy."

"I'm sorry, what?"

The room flipped over, the ceiling opening like a

tunnel and tipping me out. Once again, I fell out and landed in a sprawling heap, this time on the lobby floor.

Estelle exclaimed, the pixie flying around her head in dizzying circles. "There you are. I worried you got stuck in a cage as well."

The answer lies with his enemy. Did Evangeline know where the Grim Reaper was?

My head kept spinning for a moment before I used the desk to pull myself upright. "I think I need to visit Evangeline."

"Why?" Her eyes widened. "Does she know who's responsible for the curse?"

"No idea, but the Grim Reaper *paid* her a visit before he left town, and *he* might have known. The Room implied she knows where he is."

"Wow." Estelle coaxed the pixie to calm down and sit on her shoulder. "Are you positive she'll tell you, though?"

"Nope." It was early evening by now, an ideal time to pay the vampires a visit. Admittedly, there was never a *good* time to go and tick off the leader of the vamps, but no other routes to the Grim Reaper remained. Whether Xavier would agree was another matter entirely, but perhaps I could take Laney with me instead. Evangeline would try to play games with me either way. Going alone didn't strike me as a good idea, so I sent Xavier a message asking him to meet me at the vampires' place as soon as possible.

In the meantime, I went looking for Laney. Cass was nowhere to be seen, but Laney emerged from the shadows when I entered the living room.

"There you are," she said. "Estelle said you got stuck in a book."

"It happens." I sat down on the sofa, still mildly dizzy from Sylvester's trickery with the Forbidden Room. "I did find out one thing: Evangeline *does* know where to find the Grim Reaper."

"So you want to see her?" Laney asked. "Why would he tell his immortal enemy and not his apprentice?"

"I have no idea," I said. "I got the answer from the Book of Questions, so it has to be accurate."

I trusted the owl more than I did the vampires' leader or the Grim Reaper, but I couldn't say for sure that his advice wouldn't blow up in my face.

"Want me to come with you?" she asked.

"I don't want her to play mind games with you." I paused. "But I don't want to go there alone, and Xavier is still helping the police comb through Nero's friends' possessions."

"You just need the Grim Reaper's location, right?" she said. "She'd be more willing to part with that information than something more sensitive."

"True," I said. "I know I'm more likely to get derailed by her than you are, but we have to remember not to get sucked into any vampire mind games."

"I won't get under your feet," she said. "I'll be your backup like old times."

Questioning the leading vampire was a bit different to our occasional adventures as teenagers, but I couldn't deny it was nice to have my best friend back. We headed into the lobby, where Estelle was in the process of putting the Book of Questions away.

"Can you let your mum know where I am whenever she comes back?" I asked. "We're going to see if Evangeline is feeling generous."

"Sure," she said. "I can't promise she won't freak out, though."

"It's not the first time I've taken the risk," I reminded her. "Besides, the Grim Reaper told her his location for a reason."

"Not sure I trust him either," she said. "Good luck, though."

Laney and I left the library and made our way across the square. It was already growing dark, the streetlamps casting the alleyways in shadow and bringing an unpleasant reminder of the night we'd found the dead wizard who'd unintentionally started all this. The darkness grew more complete the closer we got to the church where the vampires made their home. I hadn't set foot in there since Evangeline's party had ended in a vampire's death... and Laney had turned out to be the culprit.

She'd been trying to protect me by killing the vampires who'd sought to bring about my death, but after being turned herself, she'd had little chance but to accept Evangeline's protection. After all, if the other vamps found out she'd killed several of their own, being a vampire wouldn't save her from their wrath. For that reason, both of us were automatically indebted to her, and it'd take some skilful talking to wrangle the Grim Reaper's location from her.

Upon reaching the church, I knocked on the door. I didn't have to wait long before the leader of the vampires answered, her brows rising at the sight of the pair of us.

"Interesting," she said. "I did wonder if you'd show your face here, Aurora."

Of course she knew where the Grim Reaper was the whole

time. She'd visited Xavier solely to toy with both of us, and I wasn't having any of it.

"I heard you were the last person to see the Grim Reaper before he left town," I said bluntly. "I'd appreciate it if you told me where he is, and also if he left any information with you about how to handle the curse which is currently loose in town."

"I thought the curse had been dealt with."

A likely story. Unless she'd refrained from reading anyone's mind in the last few days, she couldn't be completely oblivious to the new spate of deaths.

"The Grim Reaper removed the curse from the first victim, but he left town afterwards," I said. "Unfortunately, the person who used the curse seems to have done the same again, so I'd appreciate your help finding the Grim Reaper."

"There's nothing I can do to stop this curse," she said. "As for the Grim Reaper, I believe his location should be between him and his apprentice."

"You know perfectly well he didn't even tell Xavier where he went." All the cards were on the table now, and I had the sinking feeling she'd drawn the winning hand from the get-go. "Believe me, I wouldn't come here and ask you if I had another option."

"I don't doubt that, Aurora." Her smile ignited a spark of anger within me, and my hands curled into fists. "Yet I cannot give you that information... not for free, at least."

What did she want? I refused to part ways with the journal, but what else of value could I possibly offer her? Laney shifted beside me, and a jolt of alarm replaced my anger. If she sacrificed herself for my sake, I'd never forgive myself.

"Can I owe you a favour?" I asked. "To be claimed at a later date?"

Would Evangeline go for that? My instincts told me no, but to my surprise, she smiled, a delighted, smug smile. "I think that will suffice, Aurora."

I dreaded to think what kind of favour she'd request from me, but that was a problem for another day. I fought to keep the relief off my face as I waited expectantly for her answer.

"All right," I said. "Will you tell me where the Grim Reaper is now?"

She gave me a fanged smile. "The Grim Reaper is staying at a place called Grim House. Xavier will know where it is, I'm sure."

Her grin widened, her gaze fixed at a spot over my shoulder, before she vanished back into the church.

I rotated on my heel. Xavier stood behind me, a stunned expression on his face.

12

"**R**ory," said Xavier. "Did she just say what I thought she did?"

"She told me where to find your boss," I said. "Have you heard of a place called Grim House?"

"I have," he said slowly. "But... this makes no sense. Why would he not tell me he was there?"

"I don't know, but we can confront him in person now we know where he is, can't we?" I asked. "Or—I suppose it's against the rules to tell me where this Grim House place is, right?"

"Yes, but this is an emergency." Xavier's voice brimmed with concern. "You promised her a favour?"

"I didn't expect it to work, but I didn't have any other ideas." I directed my response at Laney as well as him. "Short of endangering my loved ones or giving up the journal. I can't see her asking me for any favours that I'm not capable of, so I'll worry about that later."

Laney's mouth pulled. "I doubt she'd ask you to

commit murder, Rory. She's more than capable of doing that herself."

"Murder isn't the only crime she might ask you to commit," said Xavier. "However, we need to find the Grim Reaper. If he knows how to stop the curse…"

"He did remove it from the first victim," I said. "Did you find the source?"

"No, but I didn't get through all of the suspects' possessions before I got your message," he said. "I didn't tell Edwin I was going to find my boss, but I'd rather get it out of the way."

"I'll go with you." I turned to Laney. "Can you head back to the library and let Estelle know?"

"No problem." She flashed me a fanged smile which was unintentionally reminiscent of Evangeline. "Good luck, Rory."

When she vanished from sight, I turned back to Xavier. "If you'd rather go alone, I'd understand."

"No," he said. "This is your business too. You're a part of this now."

True, but breaking the Reapers' rules came with consequences, and being indebted to Evangeline was a risky enough venture. Still, it was the Grim Reaper's own fault for vanishing in the first place, and he was going to be enraged even if Xavier tracked him down alone. I'd rather Xavier didn't become the sole target for his anger.

I met his eyes. "Let's go."

He took my arm, and we stepped through the shadows and emerged a moment later on a dark street. I could barely make out our surroundings, but from the length of the street and the small number of buildings, I'd guess it to be more of a village than a town.

Xavier led the way down to a stone house which stood at the very end of the street, dark fields bordering its right-hand side.

"Grim House is an anonymous meeting point for Reapers," he said. "Not that the locals know, of course. It doesn't surprise me that Evangeline is aware of its location, though I'd prefer that she wasn't."

I took his hand and squeezed it. "Ready?"

"Sure." He pushed on the door, opening it, and we stepped into a darkened hallway.

At first, the hallway remained deserted. Then the Grim Reaper appeared, his huge, shadowy form towering over both of us. "You, Aurora, are one of the most troublesome humans I've ever had the misfortune to meet."

My heart plummeted into my shoes. "Excuse me? I'm not responsible for putting a curse on anyone. Nor am I the person who removed said curse and then ran out of town and let the killer claim two more victims. Maybe more. Rather than flinging the blame at me, can you at least tell us how to get rid of the curse?"

The Grim Reaper let me finish my speech before saying, "I believe the best way to rid Ivory Beach of the curse is to prevent *you* from returning there, Aurora."

The door slammed behind me, and my heart gave another lurch. "I have no idea what you're talking about."

Was he playing a joke? Surely not. The Grim Reaper had zero sense of humour, and besides, there was nothing remotely funny about this situation.

"Grim Reaper." Xavier spoke from beside me, the faint glow of his scythe the only source of light. "Leave Rory alone. We need you to tell us how to stop the killer."

"The easiest way is to remove the target, is it not?"

My throat went dry. *I* was the target?

"You think the killer was after Rory?" Xavier said in disbelieving tones.

"How could I possibly be the target?" I asked. "The first victim… I was nowhere near him when he died."

"The killer intended Xavier to pick up his soul, but I went there myself, since the two of you were… occupied." A note of distaste entered his voice. "What I found was a man with a lethal curse on him, so I removed it myself."

"Then you disappeared." My throat tightened. *It can't have been aimed at me.* "How did you know I was the target?"

"You didn't," said Xavier. "You can't have. But you still left town without telling either of us that someone had used a lethal curse and was likely to strike again."

"That type of curse is too complex to be used more than once," he said.

"Clearly, someone did exactly that." I wrapped my arms around myself, shivering uncontrollably. "Why'd they go after the staff at the hospital?"

"To get at your aunt," Xavier said from the darkness beside me. "Right?"

"Precisely," said the Grim Reaper. "However, that group of meddling outsiders insisted on getting in the way and picking up the curse themselves."

Nero the Wonder and his friends.

"How do you know all this?" I asked. "Have you been sneaking in and out of town without telling anyone? Even your apprentice?"

"Xavier knows the world does not revolve around him," he said. "As for you?"

"You just told me I was the killer's target." Anger overtook my shock and disbelief. "Do you know *who* the killer is?"

"If I did, then I would have informed you," he said.

"No, you wouldn't have." I folded my arms, glaring at him. Not that he could see my face. "I assumed you were too ancient and clever to be petty enough to avoid your apprentice due to your own stubbornness, but I guess not."

"I would advise you not to push your luck, Aurora."

My hands trembled, but I kept going. "If you planned to confront the killer, why'd you spend the past few days hiding in here instead? You can walk through shadows, so I'm pretty sure tracking a murderer isn't beyond you."

"It is against the rules for me to intervene." His voice echoed in the dark hallway. "As it is against the rules for Xavier to consort with humans."

"You *did* intervene with the first victim," said Xavier. "You removed the curse. If you'd remained totally impartial, then you would have left it to run its course."

"Exactly," I said. "You can't keep needling Xavier about the Reapers' rules and then bend them yourself whenever it's convenient."

"Besides," Xavier said, "you can hardly pin the blame on Rory for not knowing she was the killer's target if you elected not to inform her yourself. How long have you known?"

"What if my family members had been targeted by accident?" How many close calls had we had? "Are you so angry with me for dating your apprentice that you'd rather I *died?*"

"If I wanted you dead, Aurora, then I would not need to resort to such indirect means to take your life."

Didn't I know it. "You certainly went out of your way to avoid letting me know. Unless you were so fixated on your own anger with Xavier that you were willing to ignore everything else."

For a moment, I feared I'd gone too far and expected to feel the cold press of the scythe on my neck. A moment passed before the Grim Reaper said, "That is not why I came here."

"Then why?" Xavier asked. "It had better be important."

"The Reaper Council requested a report from me," he said. "If they realise that my apprentice has been sharing our secrets with a human, then they will take steps. I would be surprised if they didn't immediately remove Xavier from this region and send him somewhere else."

The world swayed beneath my feet. That was almost worse than taking away his apprenticeship altogether. At least then he'd have the choice to stay in Ivory Beach. But to be reassigned to another region and simply vanish from my life? "You *told* them—"

"No, I did not," he said. "But that is why I opted against bringing you with me, Xavier. I can no longer trust you to be impartial. The fact that you brought a human here with you is further proof of that."

"You forced my hand." Xavier's words were measured, but a slight tremor underlaid his voice. "If I *am* reassigned, then you're equally to blame."

"Exactly." My eyes burned, and I clenched my jaw. "Given your behaviour, you have serious nerve to lecture Xavier about acting too much like a human."

"If you lock Rory in here to keep the curse from

spreading, that still counts as interference," Xavier added. "It's not an impartial action. Let us go."

The darkness shifted around us. I held my breath, and a clicking sound came from behind me. Xavier caught my arm and whispered, "The door's open."

I swiftly reached the door before the Grim Reaper changed his mind, escaping into the night. Xavier joined me a moment later. His mouth was pulled taut, and even his aquamarine eyes seemed darker than usual.

I blinked hard, leaning close to him. "Don't listen to him, Xavier."

"I won't." His hand found mine. "You shouldn't either. He didn't give us away to the Council."

"That doesn't mean they won't keep pushing." A tear leaked from my eye. "If you're reassigned..."

Xavier would have to choose his apprenticeship over me. I wouldn't force him to give up being a Reaper, but the notion of him leaving again drove a knife into my chest.

"I won't be." He pulled me against him, his embrace strong, steady. "Trust me."

"I do." My lips met his for a brief second. Then we stepped through the shadows and landed on the library's doorstep. "Where are you...?"

"I'll go back to help Edwin at the police station," he said. "There can't be that many objects left to go through. I might not know how to remove the curse myself, but I can at least help to stop it from affecting anyone else."

Maybe I was as self-centred as the Grim Reaper claimed, but I didn't think it was unreasonable for him to have at least told Xavier how to remove the curse from its source. While I was reluctant to leave him, I needed to tell my family that I'd been the killer's target all along.

One hug goodbye later and I entered the library alone. I found Laney where I'd left her, on the sofa in the family's living quarters, and she bounded to her feet when she saw me.

"Did you find him?" she asked.

"Yes." I rubbed my eyes. "Apparently, *I'm* the killer's target, though."

"Wait, what?" she asked. "*You're* the one the curse was supposed to be aimed at?"

"Allegedly," I said. "The Grim Reaper was so mad at us for tracking down the secret Reaper hideout that he refused to offer any help, so I have no idea how to *stop* the curse. He said it shouldn't have been possible for the killer to use it twice, but plainly they did exactly that."

Who on earth had I made an enemy of who had access to deadly curses, though? Not the Founders, surely, but I was short on any other ideas.

"That's bizarre," said Laney. "Who's trying to bump you off using a curse? Have you talked to all of Nero the Wonder's friends? Maybe one of them got really mad at you for not taking his poetry seriously."

I snorted despite myself. "If it was, they were pretty careless, considering they hit one of their own people as well. The only other possible culprit is Professor Colt, but he claimed his interest was purely theoretical."

"Might have been an act, though," she said. "You'd think the Grim Reaper would have at least told you the culprit."

"He said he didn't know," I said. "He claimed he would have interfered if he did, but that led to a messy argument about the Reapers' non-interference rule which ended in him implying that the Reaper Council might send Xavier to another region if they found out about our relationship."

"I thought he already got over that," said Laney.

"Apparently not," I said. "The funny thing is, his disappearance directly led to Xavier sharing more secret Reaper information with me, like the location of their hideout. He brought it on himself."

Movement in the corner of my eyes indicated Sylvester watching us, his owl form perched atop the door frame.

I rose to my feet. "Back in a second."

Her brow wrinkled when she caught sight of the owl, but she didn't rise to her feet to follow me. "Sure."

I walked into the lobby, expecting Sylvester to fly after me. Sure enough, he swooped away from the door and landed on a nearby shelf. "You do have a knack for trouble, don't you?"

"Tell me you didn't know I was the killer's target." He was silent for a second too long. *"Sylvester."*

"I didn't *know*," said the owl. "I merely suspected."

"Thanks for telling me." My bad mood came roaring back. "Honestly. I suppose you knew where the Grim Reaper was too."

"I am not privy to that information, which is why I sent you to the vampire instead," he said. "And she told you, did she not?"

"Yes, but—Sylvester, what if one of the others had got hit by the curse instead of me? You should have told us."

"There was no evidence," he said. "Simply conjecture

on my part, and the killer's obvious ineptitude didn't help matters."

"Ineptitude? Three people are still dead." I paced down the shelf, anger coursing through me. "Can you at least tell me where the cursed object is?"

"Ask the room at midnight."

I made a rude gesture at the owl. "I wouldn't touch your room with a ten-foot wand."

"Wands aren't ten feet long, you buffoonish toadstool." He flew away into the darkness, not without clipping me with his wing on the way.

"What did you do to deserve that?" Cass walked into view, a book tucked under her arm.

I stifled a groan, hoping she hadn't heard the rest of our conversation. "Sylvester was being obnoxious."

"Did he catch you in a room with your Reaper boyfriend?"

"I'm sorry, what?" Where would she even get that idea? "He decided not to tell me that the killer has been trying to get at *me* the whole time. I had to ask the Grim Reaper of all people."

Cass tilted her head. "This I've got to hear."

"We found the Grim Reaper," I said. "Allegedly, he was at a private meeting with the Reaper Council, but I'm more inclined to think he was hiding from his apprentice because they had an argument."

"About you?" she said. "Don't look at me like that. I know the Grim Reaper's got his robe in a tangle about the two of you even if he claims otherwise, so it figures that he went for a sulk."

"Without telling me there was a killer after me." I began pacing again. "Instead of actually pointing us towards the culprit, he dropped a bunch of vague threats about Xavier suffering the consequences for intervening in human affairs. Then he threw me out."

"It's lucky he didn't do worse."

"You think I don't know that?" I stopped mid-pace. "It's not my fault the Grim Reaper lost his mind over his apprentice having a relationship with a human."

"I doubt that was the catalyst."

"He pretty much told me it was."

"Like he's not capable of lying?" She fixed her gaze on me. "You know what I think? He removed the curse from the first victim and unintentionally saved your life in the process, and then he freaked out because it made him look like he cares about his apprentice after all. That's the real reason he's mad at you both."

"Is he capable of caring about anyone?" He certainly treated the Reapers' rules as far more flexible than I'd ever been aware, but if he'd saved my life for Xavier's sake, it explained why he'd had a sudden moment of panic. Not that he'd ever admit it. "Whatever the case, we still have a killer to find."

"Then we'll catch them," said Cass. "Mark my words."

13

W hile Cass's unexpected pep talk kept me sustained overnight, all my worries came flooding back the following morning when I woke up to the notable absence of Sylvester's singing. I guessed he was still irked with me about the incident in the Forbidden Room the previous day.

The library was due to reopen that morning, since no evidence had been found that any traces of the curse might have lingered in the library itself. But neither had the killer been caught, while I had yet to hear word from Xavier as to whether his boss had got over his temper tantrum enough to come back to town and start doing his job again.

As for my family? So far, only Cass knew I was supposedly the killer's target, since Aunt Adelaide had reportedly stayed in the high-security part of the library until the early hours of the morning and hadn't even emerged at dinnertime. Estelle, meanwhile, had thrown herself into another all-nighter with her thesis to make up for the time she'd lost yesterday, while Aunt Candace and Cass were as reclusive as ever.

Since nobody else was around, I made myself breakfast downstairs and then got out my dad's journal, but the idea of going back to reading about Reapers after the previous night's events was not an appealing one. The image of the Grim Reaper towering over me and hurling threats in my direction made me break out in shivers, so I closed the journal and returned to my breakfast instead.

Aunt Adelaide entered the kitchen as I was finishing off my coffee. "Oh, hello, Rory."

I put down my coffee mug. "There you are. I was starting to worry."

My aunt looked as though she'd hardly slept, with dark circles under her eyes and her hair as unkempt as Aunt Candace's. "I lost track of time in the high-security section. Literally. Those rooms can be very temperamental, and I'm sorry to say that I didn't find out anything substantial about the curse."

"I did, though." Where to even start? "I was going to tell you yesterday, but you weren't around. I asked the Book of Questions where to find the Grim Reaper in the hopes that *he* might be able to help."

She paused in the act of pouring herself a mug of coffee. "The Book told you where he was?"

"No, the book told me Evangeline knew, and *she* told me." I put my head in my hands. "That's when it went all wrong."

"You didn't promise her anything in return... did you?"

"A favour." It'd seemed like a worthy trade-off at the time, but now? I wasn't so sure. "I didn't want to give her the journal, and I had no other ideas."

"Of course," she said gently. "As for the favour… if it wasn't specific, it might be no big deal at all. If she wants something from the library, she won't be able to use it to cause any trouble."

"I thought—well, I hoped that'd be the case," I said. "I wish there'd been another way, but there wasn't. The Grim Reaper seemed to have no intention of showing his face."

"You did find him?" she asked.

"We did," I said. "At some kind of secret Reaper hide-out. He claimed he went there to give a report to the Reaper Council, but he completely flipped out when Xavier and I showed up. He claimed that *I* was the killer's target and that he removed the curse from the first victim and assumed that was the end of it."

"You mean Rufus?" Her eyes rounded. "How can you have possibly been the target, Rory? That doesn't make any sense."

"It didn't to me until he told us that Xavier was supposed to move Rufus's soul to the afterlife, and I was meant to run headfirst into the curse," I explained. "Instead, the Grim Reaper broke the curse and then got rid of the evidence before disappearing."

"The killer struck again, though."

"Yeah." I ducked my head, a fresh wave of shame washing over me at the recollection of yesterday's events. "At the hospital… you were supposed to be the target. I think you were supposed to bring the curse back to the library."

"*Me?*" She sucked in a breath. "I thought the curse wasn't on the library book."

"That's the part we're stuck on. The Grim Reaper

knows what's been going on while he was away, but not where the curse was used the second time."

"I thought Mr Bennet was supposed to be helping the police," she said.

"And Xavier, since he's the only person who can touch the cursed object without dropping dead." I pulled out my phone. "My phone signal is acting up again, so I don't know if he's found the source yet or if the Grim Reaper has told him how to remove the curse. He hasn't contacted me since last night."

"The Grim Reaper knew you were the target all along," she said. "Why did he assume removing the curse once would prevent the killer from trying again?"

"I'm more surprised that he intervened the first time around," I said. "It's not allowed, according to their rules, but to be honest, I think it's almost impossible *not* to interfere in some manner. Nobody can be completely impartial."

And if the Grim Reaper *had* once been impartial, then something had changed. Perhaps it was his apprentice's influence, or perhaps Cass was right and we'd both played a part, especially Xavier.

"No, you're right." She finished pouring her coffee and stuck some bread in the toaster. "The library will reopen as usual today, but if you feel unsafe…"

"I don't, but I also don't want anyone else to get hit by the curse in my place if it's still at large," I said. "The killer doesn't seem to want to come near me in person."

"Hmm." Her worried gaze went to my dad's journal, and once again, I found myself wondering if this somehow went back to the Founders and their long-standing grudge against my dad and me. "It does seem rather a half-hearted effort on their part, if no less dangerous even so."

"Yeah." I picked up the journal and translator document and slipped them back into my bag.

"Were you working on that?" asked Aunt Adelaide. "Oh, you've made some progress, I see."

"Laney helped me with some of it yesterday." Yet another thing I hadn't had the chance to tell her yet. I figured it was time to stop being paranoid about Evangeline reading the journal's secrets from Laney's thoughts. Good timing, considering now I owe her a favour.

"Oh, I'm glad you and Laney aren't letting the vampires drive a wedge between the two of you," she said. "Did you learn anything interesting?"

"My dad first met the vampires on a trip to Europe when he was hunting down a rare book," I said. "I think the vampires were after the same book, but… but he didn't want to risk bringing trouble on the library."

Aunt Adelaide's lips pressed together. "I understand why he never told us of his history with the vampires, but I sometimes wish he had."

"Did he ever mention meeting a Reaper?"

"A Reaper?" She broke off as the phone started ringing. "I'll get that."

As she did so, I took the journal with me to the front desk to prepare to open the library for the day, since it was almost nine o'clock. In truth, I was hardly in the mood to deal with the public, but the quicker we got back to some semblance of normality after yesterday, the better it would be for the library as a whole.

I scowled when I found the Book of Questions sitting on the desk and pointedly moved it to another shelf, out of sight. You'd think Sylvester might have been nice enough to hint that I was the killer's target, but the *Grim Reaper* had been more helpful, despite his general unpleasantness yesterday.

I turned back to the journal, fighting past my reluctance. Until Xavier returned and confirmed the curse had been removed, I needed to make the most of the time I had. I didn't need to replace my fear of Evangeline with a new wariness around the journal due to my dad's history with the Reapers. Besides, what if the journal pointed me to a way to resolve my current dilemma?

I laid the translated document on the desk and read on: *A shadow follows me even at home.*

My throat went dry, but I forced myself to continue. *I've seen it a few times, though it always disappears whenever I try to take a close look. As for the book I acquired, it's certainly a wondrous piece of art, if incomprehensible to me since I can't read the ancient language.*

The journal entries then skipped forward several days before continuing.

The shadow finally showed its face today when it caught me alone on my way home from work.

"You didn't listen to me," said the Reaper. "I told you not to anger the vampires."

I hadn't seen any signs of the vampires since I'd left the village with the book in my hands, but I have to admit it unnerved me that the Reaper had followed me all the way home.

"Why would you warn me in the first place?" I asked.

"Those vampires are my enemies," he replied. "And now they are yours too."

I might have asked him any number of questions. Instead, I simply asked, "Why?"

"Have you ever heard of the Founders before?" he asked. "Be glad if you haven't, but they are a ruthless sect who will not hesitate to use any means by which to secure what they want. You have a family, don't you? Your wife is a normal, and you have a young child."

"How dare you!" My heart had begun to race at his words. There was no reason for him to give me such a warning. "What would you have me do? Give the book to them? I have no idea who these Founders are or where I might find them, if I ever wanted to."

"You have somewhere safe to hide the book, don't you?"

Yes. The library was as safe as it was possible to be, but the notion of putting Adelaide and the others in danger lay heavily on my conscience. Besides, if I returned to the library myself, its magic might try to force me to stay, which wouldn't be fair to Rory.

My only alternative would be to leave it with someone else in Ivory Beach, someone who would understand the need for secrecy. It's not ideal, but I cannot continue to keep the book in my house or in the bookshop as long as these Founders are looking for it.

I might not know why the Reaper warned me, but I know better than not to heed his advice.

I lifted my head, my heart racing. If he'd gone to hide the book in Ivory Beach, had the rest of the family known he'd returned? I jumped to my feet when Aunt Adelaide walked back into the lobby.

"Rory?" she said. "I'm afraid I have bad news. There's been another victim of the curse."

"Who?"

"I'm not sure," she said. "Someone who was present in

the jail at the time. I'm going to speak to Edwin in person and find out more."

"Wait." I came out from behind the desk, alarmed. "If I'm the target, we can't risk any of us getting closer to the victim in case the curse tries to make the jump."

"I'm not sure you *are* the killer's target, Rory," she said. "Is it possible the Grim Reaper was mistaken?"

"Maybe, but I don't see how he would be." He'd removed the curse the first time around, though he hadn't told Xavier how to do it. "I'm going to speak to Xavier and see if his boss has got in touch. One of them must have removed the victim's soul."

I'd have to run straight there without interacting with anyone else, but that sounded easier than keeping an eye on everyone in my family at once.

"Right," said Aunt Adelaide. "I'll go to the—"

A deafening crash sounded from upstairs, followed by cackling laughter that sounded awfully like Sylvester.

"What has that owl done now?" Aunt Adelaide made for the stairs while I found myself wondering the same. I'd feel more secure if my aunt and the others didn't leave the library, but Sylvester wouldn't have tried to distract her for that reason, would he?

I called my familiar. "Jet, can you check on the others and let them know that the killer is still at large and might target any of them as well as the library? I'm going to see if the Grim Reaper will deign to tell me how to stop the curse."

"Yes, partner!" The little crow swooped around, yelling, "Danger, danger!"

"Maybe tone it down a little," I said. "Just be firm and don't let anyone in."

In the meantime, I left the library, hoping I wasn't making a mistake by going outside at all. I crossed the square and made straight for the graveyard, scarcely stopping to take a breath until I reached the gates leading to the Reaper's house.

While nobody waited behind the fence this time around, a chill pursued me all the way to the door. Before I lost my nerve, I used the old-fashioned door knocker, and an echoing boom resounded in the air.

The door opened, and a shadow filled my vision, the towering form of the Grim Reaper filling the entire corridor with darkness.

"You're back." My thoughts tumbled over another in my mind. "But that means…"

"Yes, I am," he said. "And my apprentice has gone."

14

I stared up at the Grim Reaper. "What do you mean, gone?"

"Is the word not self-explanatory?"

"Not to me." This couldn't be possible. "When did you get back?"

"I fail to see how that is relevant in the slightest, Aurora."

"If Xavier is gone, then when did he leave?" Had he taken off because of the way his boss had treated him? Or had he been targeted by the killer? "Haven't you looked for him?"

"I have searched everywhere within my power," he said. "Now, leave."

What does that mean? Xavier was immune to curses, and I couldn't imagine anyone getting the upper hand on the Reaper, but while he was distracted and angry, he might have fallen into any kind of trap.

I have to find him.

I turned my back on the house and left the graveyard,

panic rising inside me. If Xavier had left using his shadow-travel ability, he might have gone anywhere, but it seemed out of character for him to run off of his own accord. On the other hand, if he'd been taken by the enemy instead, that still left too many possible places he might be and with precious few clues as to who the culprit had been in the first place.

The only logical place to start was the police station, so I retraced my steps towards the square and headed to the seafront. I found the police station as crowded as the last time I'd been there, with Edwin's trolls struggling to hold back a crowd of Nero the Wonder's friends from entering the doors to the jail at the back.

I had to admit that part of me had briefly wondered if he and his friends had somehow cornered Xavier in order to convince him to undo the curse, but it couldn't be plainer that the Reaper was nowhere in sight. Instead, the elf policeman was making a valiant attempt to gain control over the chaos, but nobody would listen to a word he said.

"What's going on this time?" I made my way over to Edwin, who hovered behind the desk with an expression which implied he'd be happier inside a cell himself. "Did someone really die in here?"

"No," he said. "Who told you that?"

"I thought you called my aunt." I frowned. "Have you seen Xavier, then?"

"No, I haven't." He raised his voice over the ruckus from the back of the lobby. "I've been a little preoccupied. We opted to keep some of the major suspects in cells overnight, more for their own safety than anything. They kept trying to retrieve their confiscated possessions."

"Did you ask the curse-breaker to check everything you confiscated from them?" I asked. "Or—wait, did Xavier finish checking them himself?"

"Yes, but there's a slight issue," he said. "None of the items we confiscated was cursed."

My heart skipped a beat. "So one of them must still have the object, or at least know where it is."

"That's what I thought," he said. "Unfortunately, we have yet to get a straight answer out of anyone. They only seem to be concerned for their idol."

"You thought Nero the Wonder was the likely culprit?"

"He's their ringleader," he said. "And he was hiding recording equipment in his clothing, as we found out when we searched him."

"Of course he was." I grimaced. "Maybe I can try talking to him. Something is odd about this whole situation."

Aunt Adelaide had taken a call telling her someone had died, but if Edwin denied making the call, had someone been trying to lure her outside? Had they done so from here while Edwin was distracted with Nero the Wonder's friends? Since the majority of my suspects were inside this very prison, the odds were all too high.

Edwin gave me a weary look. "I shouldn't let you, but why do I get the feeling you've been keeping information from me, Aurora?"

"The curse-breaker and the Grim Reaper kept information from all of us," I said. "They were the ones who took care of the curse that killed Rufus. I'm guessing Mr Bennet didn't tell you that?"

His lips compressed. "How long have you known?"

"Not long," I said. "I don't know whereabouts the curse

is this time around or who is responsible, but the Grim Reaper himself told me I was the intended target."

"*You?*" He blinked. "I suppose one doesn't easily dismiss a warning from a Reaper."

"Exactly," I said. "Anyway, can I please speak to Nero the Wonder?"

"Fine." He beckoned to one of his troll guards. "Can you escort Aurora to Nero's cell? She believes she might be able to convince him to give away some pertinent information."

I had little confidence in my powers of persuasion, but I had to admit part of me expected to find Xavier hiding in the jail and conducting an interrogation of his own. Instead, the jail appeared to be more or less deserted, though several of Nero's friends tried to follow me through, and a series of crashes and shouts filled the background as the troll escorted me to his cell.

The Wonder sat on a bench, his arms folded across his chest, and grunted when he saw me. "Can you believe they took away my wand?"

"Which object was the curse on?" I asked, deciding to get straight to the point. "You must know. Did Nera touch anything?"

"I don't know about any curse," he said. "I'm not lying. You can't keep me locked up in here."

"I'm not responsible for locking you up," I said. "But your fans are out of control. If you just tell the police what you know, then you can all leave, and everyone will be glad of it."

He worked his jaw. "If I tell you what you want to know, will you let me leave?"

"If Edwin says so, yes, but you have to tell me the truth."

"There's no curse," he said.

My heart missed a beat. "What?"

"Told you, there isn't a curse," he said. "That's not what killed Nera."

"Then what did?"

"Poison," he said. "I smelled it on her. It's called Sudden Death. I only know the name because we filmed an episode of my show a few months ago where I conjured up a few bottles of deadly poison and juggled them."

Seriously? His manner was sombre enough that I was inclined to believe him, but his words raised an entirely different set of questions. "How did nobody find any traces of the poison on Nera's body, then?"

"No idea," he said. "It's bright pink. You can't miss it."

Weird. I thought back to the chaos surrounding Nera's sudden death, but I would definitely have noticed any bright-pink deadly poison, unless it'd been hidden in her hair. "I hope you're telling the truth. Do you know who the killer is?"

"No," he said. "I don't know anyone who had a bottle of poison, either. The police would have found it."

Even the Grim Reaper had said the curse couldn't be used more than once, so if the killer had used another method entirely for the other two victims, it would explain how we'd been unable to trace the cause. But how had they hidden and administered the poison? And how, if it wasn't an unpredictable curse, had they managed to hit two of the wrong targets?

I turned back to the troll guard. "I need to talk to Edwin."

"Sure." He sloped down the hallway back to the main part of the jail while I dodged Nero's friends in an effort to reach Edwin.

"Anything?" A note of hopefulness entered his tone. "Did he confess?"

"No, but he told me it's not a curse at all," I said. "Nera died from some kind of poison called Sudden Death. He recognised the scent, but it's also supposed to be bright pink."

"What?" He peered over my shoulder at his security troll, who was in the process of trying to keep Nero's followers from getting into the jail. "Not a curse? Are you sure he's telling the truth?"

"I think he is." It would explain why we hadn't found the cursed object, at any rate.

His eyes narrowed. "You mean to say I've been wasting my time?"

"I'm not sure even the curse-breaker would have guessed there wasn't a curse when that *is* what killed the first victim." Neither had the staff at the hospital, it seemed. "The killer opted to use a different route for their second attempt."

And their third, too. As for Xavier's disappearance? I couldn't say for sure if there was a connection, but I refused to believe he'd left town out of a temper tantrum like his boss had.

"Where are you going?" Edwin asked as I approached the door.

"To ask about poisons that mimic curses."

I got halfway to the library before I changed direction and headed up the high street towards the university campus instead. Driven by instinct alone, I reached the cluster of buildings comprising the university campus and nearly ran into the professor, who was coming in the opposite direction. Instinctively, I grabbed my wand, and he gave me a look of startled surprise.

"Aurora," he said. "Sorry, I didn't see you there. I'm leaving for a weekend trip… is something wrong?"

I lowered my wand but didn't put it away. "Why are you leaving in such a hurry?"

"Urgent business trip," he said. "I'll be back on Monday if you need me."

"I'd rather talk now." My grip on my wand tightened, but his expression didn't show anything other than confusion. "Do you know of a poison which can cause someone to drop dead of no apparent causes? Sudden Death?"

"My speciality is curses, not poison," he said. "I *do* know of that one, though. Why?"

"The killer used that," I said. "Not a curse at all."

"They did?" He attempted to edge around me. "I'd suggest you ask in the potions and poisons department if that's the case."

"What's this errand of yours?" If he knew nothing of the murders, why would he be acting so shifty?

"Ah, I need to go and pick up a book for safekeeping."

His words struck a chord in my mind. "Did you know my dad?"

He stilled for a moment. "Your dad?"

"Roger Hawthorn," I said. "Did he give *you* that rare book to look after? There aren't that many places outside of the library to hide a rare book where it won't stand out."

"I knew him," he said slowly. "I was sorry to hear he died. What rare book are you talking about?"

"I read his journal," I said. "That's how I know he brought it here. I know he probably told you not to tell anyone, but can't you make an exception for his daughter?"

He drew in a shuddering breath. "I suppose... but honestly, nobody could read that book. It isn't here, anyway. I sent it elsewhere for safekeeping."

"Safekeeping?" I echoed. "Isn't the campus safe?"

"Not as much as it once was," he said. "Not with certain shady individuals known to be looking for rare books. I'm afraid there's nothing more I can do to help you, Aurora."

He must mean the Founders. Before I could say another word, he hurried through the gates and out of sight, leaving me blinking after him.

Safekeeping? I entered the campus and made for his office, for the lack of any better ideas, keeping my wand in a firm grip. When I entered the office he'd vacated, it became evident he'd left in a hurry. The place was a mess, piles of books and papers littering every surface, cabinets open, desk in disarray. He'd even left the back-room door open. I walked that way and almost trod on a glass vial lying on its side, spilling a clear liquid onto the carpet.

Carefully, I crouched down to read the label on the vial. This one I actually remembered from my textbook. The vial contained a concoction to remove stains and dyes.

Like, say, the pink colour of a potion.

Drawing in a breath, I picked up the vial, careful not to spill a drop. In the same moment, the door opened, and the professor's assistant walked in. Lara spat her gum into the bin and pointed her wand in my direction.

15

W ithout taking an eye off Lara's wand, I held up the vial. "Is this yours?"

"No."

I didn't need to be able to read her mind to know that for a lie. "Well, it's someone's, and your boss has left town. Did he leave you to lock up after him?"

"Something like that." She still didn't put her wand down. "What are you doing here?"

"I thought you expected me." I abandoned all pretence. "Why did you call my aunt and pretend someone died from the curse? Were you trying to lure me outside? Because the police station is in the opposite direction from here."

She blinked again, the wand trembling in her hand. "What?"

"Why poison?" I pressed on. "Were you that reluctant to confront me directly?"

A flush rose up her neck. "Poison?"

"Yes, Sudden Death, which is usually bright pink in

colour… unless you use this to dilute it." I put the vial down on the desk. "How did you end up targeting someone at the hospital instead?"

The flush reached her face. "It should have been your aunt, but he picked up the glass of water instead."

A dozen recriminations flickered through my mind, but the pressing question was, "Why?"

"I had to do something," she said. "This scholarship is all I have. If the police even considered me as a potential suspect, they'd have taken it away from me."

"That's not what I meant." *How can she have killed three people?* "Why do you want me dead? Is it about my dad and the book he left here with the professor? The book the Founders were after?"

Her hands shook more visibly when I said the word 'Founders'. "They would have killed us if they knew we had it."

"You know their ringleaders are in jail, don't you?" I should know, because they'd tried to kill me several times and turned my best friend into a vampire before I'd put them there.

"They're a big group," she said quietly. "You've never seen the rest of the magical world outside this town, have you? The Founders killed my family and left me orphaned."

"I'm sorry for that, but the Founders already came to town, and they never came after the book," I said. "The professor said he didn't even have the book anymore, besides."

"They'll come back," she insisted. "This isn't anywhere near the end of it, Rory."

Her words brought a chill to my skin. Her fear was

understandable, but I'd seen to Mortimer Vale's imprison-
ment, and I didn't see how he could possibly give directions from behind bars.

"If they do come back for the book, it won't matter if
I'm dead or alive," I pointed out. "Unless you know where
the professor hid it?"

She shrugged one shoulder. "Does it matter?"

"If the Founders are after it, then yes." I adjusted my
grip on my wand, thinking quickly through my options.
Xavier was nowhere to be seen, my family remained
safely in the library, and the police were too occupied
keeping Nero the Wonder's friends restrained to be able
to offer me any help. That meant I needed to talk Lara out
of any drastic actions without making her panic and cause
even more havoc. She'd already killed three people in her
wild attempts to reach me without drawing too much
attention to herself.

Lara raised her wand, seeing my slight movement.
From the tremor in her fingertips, it was clear why she'd
tried a less direct means of murder that didn't involve
getting her hands dirty, but her future depended on me
not giving her away to the police. That made her
desperate.

I cast a freeze-frame spell on her while ducking to
avoid her own spell. A bolt of light shot wildly over my
head and crashed into a cabinet, sending papers flying
everywhere. My freeze-frame spell missed, too, because
she gave a catlike lunge for the door and then spun on me
again.

Instinct drove me to duck underneath the desk as she
sent a wave of clear liquid flying across the room, splat-
tering the desk and drenching every paper in sight. The

smell of something musky wafted out, making me suppress the urge to cough.

"You won't die right away," Lara told me. "From a single drop of the poison, it'll take up to twelve hours for the effects to come on."

I hardly dared to breathe as I crawled underneath the desk. By some miracle, only traces of the liquid splattered my clothes, but she might have more of the deadly poison on her.

"Nasty stuff, this," I said to her, reaching into my pocket carefully to avoid touching any of the poison. "How'd you kill that girl, then? If she didn't put her hands on anything cursed, then she must have come into contact with the poison somehow."

As I spoke, I gingerly pulled out my Biblio-Witch Inventory and shuffled out from underneath the desk.

"That was a mistake, too," she muttered. "I told her to deliver it to the library, but she must have drunk it herself."

I crouched in front of the desk, my fingers seeking the words on the pages of my Biblio-Witch Inventory. "What did you do with the Reaper, then?"

She blinked. "Reaper?"

"The Grim Reaper caught on to your first murder," I told her. "Is that why you stopped using the curse method in case it got you caught?"

The colour drained from her face. Her hesitation cost her, because I touched the word *light,* causing a blinding flash to rise from my pocket. As her hands raised to shield her eyes, I used my wand to cast the freeze-frame spell, which worked this time, halting her body mid-motion.

"If you kill me, the Reaper will show up to take my

soul." I skimmed the page for the right spell. "He can walk through walls, did you know?"

She recovered faster than I'd expected and ran out of the room, pointing her wand over her shoulder. A burst of light whipped over my shoulder and hit the cabinets with a crash and an explosion of brightness. To my horror, flames sprang up across the spilled poison on the desk as whatever had been in the cabinets ignited.

I ran for the door and found it sealed tight. She'd locked me in. Panic sparked at the sight of the fire covering the desk and the accompanying memory of the fire which had almost taken out Abe and my dad's old shop. With no access to a fire alarm, I tried a water-conjuring spell, but if anything, the flames leapt higher instead of shrinking. The unlocking spell I tried on the door didn't work, either. Eyes watering, I scanned my Biblio-Witch Inventory, conscious of the flames continuing to burn and the smoke rising from their midst. My gaze stopped on the new freezing spell Estelle had taught me. Out of any better ideas, I pressed my fingertip to the word.

To my intense relief, it worked, and the flames turned to ice. Yet the door refused to unlock no matter how many spells I used on it, while the ice wouldn't last forever. I dug my hand into my pocket and searched for my notebook, groaning when I found a handful of fire-dust underneath it. The last thing I wanted was to create *more* fire.

Then my hand closed around a smooth, cool stone. The stone Xavier had given me for me to use to contact him in an emergency. This situation definitely qualified as such.

I squeezed the stone and pictured Xavier in my mind's eye. At first, nothing happened. *Is he really gone?*

Then, shadows folded around me from behind. Xavier appeared for a heartbeat and caught my hand before the room vanished around the two of us.

I staggered back when he let go of me, and the cold shadows retreated to reveal the backdrop of the high street. So Xavier *had* been in town all along.

He looked down at me with visible concern, his attention lingering on my poison-splattered coat. "Was that a fire? Are you hurt?"

"No—wait, don't touch me. I have poison all over my clothes." My words ran together as my knees threatened to give out from sheer relief. "Lara started a fire in the professor's office, but she locked me in, and I didn't know how else to get out. We have to warn everyone."

His eyes flew wide. "I'll take us back there, and we'll set the fire alarm off."

Xavier took my hand and pulled me through shadows, and we landed in the corridor outside Professor Colt's office. Smoke was beginning to seep out from underneath the door while I sought the nearest fire alarm.

In a shatter of glass, the alarm blared out, ringing through the building. Another harried-looking professor with silver hair ran out of a nearby room. "Did Professor Colt blow up the lab again?"

"No, it was his assistant, but she ran off." The professor had apparently fire-alarm-proofed his office, no doubt due to similar experiments he'd conducted in the past. "The door is sealed from the outside with some kind of spell."

"I'll fix it," said the professor.

Thunderous footsteps echoed overhead as the alarm alerted everyone else in the building, so I ran with Xavier to the back door before we got trampled by everyone coming down from the upper floors.

"We have to find Lara." I looked for her, but there were no signs of the teenage apprentice outside the building. "She can't have gone far unless she used a transporter spell."

"I can find her." Xavier took the lead and headed across campus. "Was she the one who came to the library to speak to Estelle?"

"That's her," I said. "She's been trying to kill me half-heartedly all week because she's afraid the Founders will come after her."

"Why would the vampires come after her?" He crossed the campus, moving fast enough that I had to run to keep up.

"My dad gave the professor a book the Founders were after," I explained. "Years ago. I don't know how she found out, but the Founders killed her family, and she was terrified they'd come back."

"They're already in jail, aren't they?" Xavier said.

"That's what I told her, but she was insistent," I said breathlessly. "Never mind that. Where in the world have you been all morning? Your boss had no idea where you were."

"I went to see Evangeline," he said. "It was supposed to be a quick visit, but she insisted on keeping me waiting for hours."

"You visited her… why?"

"Because she knew where our hideout was," he said. "Vampires aren't supposed to know, and besides, I wanted to know what else she and my boss had discussed. Her response was to tell me that she had a book of yours."

"Mine?" A suspicion seized me. "Did the professor give it to her?"

Before he could answer, we reached the campus gates and found that Lara was nowhere to be seen.

"No, my boss did," he said in response to my question. "I'll tell you more later. Ready to follow her?"

"Sure." I took his hand. "Be careful—she's jumpy."

One step through the shadows later and we landed on a road out of the town, where Lara turned around with a startled cry. "You!"

"I told you the Reaper could walk through walls," I said.

Xavier approached her, scythe in hand, and she crumpled in a heap, her hands over her head in surrender. "Help!"

"I'm not going to take your soul," said Xavier. "That isn't my job. But I am going to take you to the police."

She whimpered, and she didn't resist when he took her hand and pulled her to her feet before stepping into the shadows. He came back for me a heartbeat later, and we landed outside the police station. There, Lara cowered before one of Edwin's security trolls.

"She's the killer," I told him. "If you didn't already know."

"She's also a minor," said Xavier. "Is Nero the Wonder still in there?"

"No." The troll shepherded Lara into the police station, which was notably quieter than it'd been the previous time I'd been there.

Behind the desk, Edwin raised his brows at the sight of our companion. "Who is she?"

"She's the person responsible for killing three people, but she's a minor," I explained. "While trying to kill me."

Edwin studied the whimpering teenager. "Are you sure?"

"Positive," I said. "She threw deadly poison at me, and she might be carrying more of it, so be careful."

Edwin's trolls, who'd started to advance on her, abruptly halted.

"I'll take care of it," Xavier said. "Lara, do you have any more of that poison with you?"

She gave a mute shake of her head. I doubted she'd lie under the threat of a scythe, so that was enough to convince the trolls to haul her off to a cell.

When they'd disappeared through the back door, I turned to Xavier. "Your boss was worried about you."

"Seriously?"

"Well, I'm not entirely sure, but it seemed that way," I said. "And... I'm sorry, but *he* had my dad's book? The professor gave it to the Grim Reaper for safekeeping?"

And the Grim Reaper had then given it to Evangeline? I definitely needed to have another chat with him, that was for sure.

"It's not the strangest thing I've heard in the past day," Xavier remarked. "Now... I think it's time I had a word with my boss."

16

In the end, the Grim Reaper did not invite me to his private meeting with Xavier. I should have expected as much since they clearly had a lot of issues they needed to work out between themselves which didn't involve me. With both Reapers back in town, I was more than happy to leave them to it.

The following day, Sylvester refrained from waking me up early, so I had a nice lie-in and then volunteered to work on the front desk in the hopes of stealing a few more moments alone with the journal. I'd hardly settled down when Aunt Adelaide came in with an update from the police. Apparently, the professor had reluctantly come back to town to testify against his apprentice and then intended to leave on a long sabbatical. Lara, meanwhile, would be shipped off to a junior detention centre—a sad end to her academic career, if not undeserved.

As for Nero the Wonder, he and his entourage had departed the town shortly after informing Edwin that he had no intention of buying property here after all. There'd also been a notable lack of new videos uploaded to his channel. Some said it was out of respect for the dead, but Jet brought news of a rumour that hooded figures with scythes had mysteriously shown up in the background of their recent videos.

"Serves them right for trying to throw a party in the cemetery if you ask me," I remarked to Jet, who perched on the shelf behind me. "Nice sleuthing. You haven't seen the Reaper around?"

"No, partner." He fluttered his wings and gave a squawk of surprise when the front door opened with barely a whisper and Evangeline entered the library.

I'd expected her to show her face soon, given Xavier's revelation that the Grim Reaper had entrusted her with the book Professor Colt had given him for safekeeping, but knowing she'd indirectly helped me out didn't quell my initial apprehension at the sight of her.

"Aurora," she said. "I heard of your recent accomplishments."

"Did you?" I did my best to keep my thoughts focused on the wooden surface of the desk, but it didn't matter too much if she probed into my thoughts. She wouldn't find anything in there that she didn't already know. "I heard you have something that used to belong to my dad."

Her expression betrayed no surprise, but the Grim Reaper must have given her some explanation when he'd handed it over to her. Though I had to wonder why he'd entrusted his immortal enemy with something so valuable. Or why the professor had given it to him in the first place. Until I read the rest of the journal, my knowledge of what had really transpired all those years ago would remain incomplete.

Evangeline reached into her pocket and pulled out a thick leather-bound book with a deep crimson cover engraved with runes. My mouth fell open when she laid it on the desk in front of me. This was the book my dad had risked his life for, knowingly or not, and I'd assumed she would have wanted to keep it for herself.

"This is one of the oldest books of vampire lore in existence," she said. "Hence its value to the Founders."

"Then why are you giving it to me?" I asked. "You know why my dad had to hide it, don't you?"

"He believed it painted a target on his back," she said. "Which was true at the time."

"At the time?" What was that supposed to mean? "They never came back for it, did they?"

"Exactly," she said. "While I doubt they've entirely forgotten it, they have long since moved to other targets."

"So they aren't coming back." Lara's fear hadn't been unfounded, but they'd never come to the campus. "I know Mortimer Vale wasn't the last of them, though. Are you giving me the book because you know they're still likely to come looking for it?"

"The Founders are a large group, and a widespread one," she said. "However, I can only read minds, not divine the future. Regardless of the outcome, the book is yours."

I debated handing it back to her, but what would be the point? The Founders had already made me their enemy, and they'd chased my dad long after the book had ceased to be relevant to them. Evangeline knew that as well as I did, and while I still wasn't a hundred percent sure Evangeline herself didn't support the Founders in some manner, she'd given me the book back. And she'd helped in her own roundabout way.

I tried to keep my thoughts blank, but I was sure she heard some of it anyway. All she did, though, was give me a smile and then leave the library.

As the door closed behind her, the sound of sweeping wings came from my shoulder, and Sylvester landed on the desk, nudging the book with his beak. "Ooh. This smells old. Valuable too."

"My dad bought it from a village in Germany over two decades ago," I told the owl. "Right from under the Founders' noses. Did you know Evangeline had it?"

"Certainly not," said Sylvester. "I knew the Reaper paid her a visit, yes, but it is beyond the expanse of my knowledge to understand the peculiarities of Reapers and vampires. I will store this book in the high-security area of the library."

"Tell Aunt Adelaide first," I said. "Did you get her lost in there for hours on purpose? I know it was you who caused a diversion yesterday to stop anyone from leaving the library."

"The library works in mysterious ways." And without further comment, he picked up the book in his claws and launched into flight.

As the owl disappeared overhead, a tired-looking Laney walked out of the entry to the living quarters. "Did I hear Evangeline's voice?"

"You do have good hearing," I said. "Yeah, she gave me the book back. The one the Grim Reaper gave her, but which was originally my dad's before he stored it with the professor for safekeeping. Don't ask me how *that* came about."

"I'm lost," she said. "Have you heard from Xavier yet?"

"Nope, but believe me, I'll expect an explanation from his boss," I said. "Anyway, it looks like he's stopped the disappearing act, but he's going to have to quit forbidding Xavier to intervene in human affairs after it turns out he did exactly that himself."

"No kidding," she said. "Evangeline didn't bring up the favour you owe her, though?"

"I forgot, but no, she didn't," I said. "She'll hold that one over my head until there's a rare book she really needs, I don't doubt."

That was the best-case scenario. I might not trust her, but I no longer believed her to be in league with the Founders, which made me feel a little better about leaving my best friend's vampire training in her hands.

Estelle walked out of the living quarters behind Laney, looking rather like a wild animal emerging from hibernation. "I finished my thesis!"

"You did?" I asked. "That's amazing."

"Yes!" She punched the air and high-fived Spark while the pixie enthusiastically shed glitter over the floor.

"Yippee!" Jet flew over to join Spark, the pair of them flying in circles in a bizarre kind of crow–pixie dance in mid-air.

Overhearing the ruckus, Aunt Adelaide approached us from the direction of the Reading Corner. "That's great news. You can return to the land of the living again."

"Good," I said. "Being a recluse doesn't suit you, Estelle."

"I know," she said. "I prefer being in the midst of the action, not locked away in my room."

"Good, because that job is already taken." It seemed the noise had drawn Aunt Candace downstairs too.

"I notice you haven't fallen over yourself to help us catch up on everything we fell behind on this week," Aunt Adelaide said to her sister.

"I have deadlines, too, you know," said Aunt Candace. "And I'm low on inspiration. I hoped to interview that Nero the Wonder to get some ideas."

"Honestly, it's better that you didn't." I reached into my bag and pulled out the translated pages of the journal I'd already finished with. "If you're looking for ideas, I'm done with this section if you want to have a read for yourself."

Aunt Candace's eyeballs practically fell out of her skull as she grabbed the papers. "What? You finally made some progress? I thought I'd be six feet underground before you moved past the first page."

"So did I, for a while," I said. "I only got through the first section, but I can trust you to be sensible enough not to drop any actual events from my dad's history into your books, can't I?"

"Are you sure?" Aunt Adelaide interjected. "I'd understand if you didn't want word to get out—especially to the vampires."

"The Founders aren't interested in the book mentioned in the journal anymore," I said. "According to Evangeline, anyway. That's why she gave it back. It only started my dad's rivalry with them, and I have a feeling he did a lot more to tick them off since then."

I still had close to two decades' worth of more diary entries to get through, after all.

"What book?" asked Aunt Candace. "Is it one of ours?"

"It is now that Evangeline gave it back to me," I said. "Sylvester put it in the high-security area, right, Aunt Adelaide?"

"Yes, he did," she said. "Don't look at me like that, Candace. It's written in an ancient language you won't be able to read, anyway."

"We do have a translator spell." Aunt Candace tutted. "I suppose these pages will suffice for now."

"You're welcome," I said. "If you want to return the favour, I'd appreciate it if you could convince Sylvester to leave me in peace to work on the translation once in a while."

"Can anyone convince the owl to do anything he doesn't want to?" Aunt Candace shook her head. "If you're going to insist upon reading ahead in your textbooks, though, perhaps I'll let you spend some of your magic lessons working on the journal instead."

That sounded reasonable to me. I might not want to share my dad's journal publicly, but Aunt Candace had referenced his life story in her novels beforehand, and it'd be a lot easier to get through the journal with the full cooperation of my family.

"That was a mistake," said Cass's voice from behind me as Aunt Candace retreated from sight. "Now you've given her a taste, she's going to keep hounding you for the rest."

I watched her step out from behind a nearby shelf, unsurprised that she'd been listening in. "I don't mind. The Founders already know my dad thwarted their attempts to get the book, and so does the professor. Besides, hoarding knowledge is the Founders' thing, not ours."

"You make a good point," said Aunt Adelaide. "Though

we'll need to be careful Evangeline didn't purposefully return that book to us in order to make us indebted to her."

I'm already indebted to her. How that would turn out for me remained to be seen.

The others scattered while I remained behind the front desk, waiting for the library to open. As the clock struck nine, however, the first person to enter the library was Xavier. My heart flipped over at the sight of him.

"You can take the rest of the morning off," said Aunt Adelaide. "You've earned it, Rory."

"Thanks." I grabbed my bag and made for the door before Cass could aim a snide comment in my direction, though she was keeping that kind of thing to a minimum these days. Stranger and stranger.

I took Xavier's hand as we left the library. "Does your boss want to give me a lecture?"

"I hope it isn't a lecture, but he does want to clear a few things up," he said. "Don't worry, you're not in trouble."

"But are you?"

"I'm his apprentice," he said. "It'd be unusual for him not to be annoyed at me for something. He has to live with me, after all."

"True, but that doesn't give him the right to be so controlling," I said. "And as for the way he acted towards us at Grim House... I hope he has something resembling an apology. And an explanation."

Xavier and I walked to the cemetery, entering via the gates and approaching the house. Xavier unlocked the door and led me into the hallway, and my heart flipped over when I saw the Grim Reaper standing inside the room on the left-hand side. He still scared the crap out of me, I'd freely admit, but he hadn't got out his scythe yet. That was a promising sign.

"Aurora," he said. "Come in."

I entered the room, mentally bracing myself. Xavier stood at my side when I sat at the table, offering silent support. I had no idea which question to start with, so I voiced the first that came to mind: "Why did the professor give you the book?"

"Because I was the only person in Ivory Beach who knew its value and who might have been able to stand up to those who sought it out," said the Grim Reaper.

"And then you gave it to Evangeline... why?" I asked. "I'm surprised you trusted Evangeline to hold onto something that valuable."

"Trust has nothing to do with my decision," he said. "I inferred from past events that Evangeline was the best equipped to deal with a potential threat from the Founders while I was absent."

"And not us?" I raised a brow. "Don't get me wrong, Evangeline is capable, but she's not exactly friendly with my family. The book originally belonged to my dad, even if the Founders saw it as rightfully theirs at one time."

"Would your family have appreciated it if I'd entered the library and given them the book in person?"

"Uh..." *Probably not.* Though I suspected the real answer was that he hadn't wanted to alert anyone to his presence before he'd left town for his trip to Grim House. "Still. My family has fought off the Founders more than once. We're the reason three of their ringleaders are in jail."

"That is true," he said. "I'm starting to see why Evangeline desires your support."

"Is that supposed to be a compliment?" The idea of having two indestructible immortals fighting over who got to claim my loyalty wasn't appealing, but it was a little better than being their enemy.

"No, it is not," said the Grim Reaper. "I hope that clears up the matter, however."

"Some of it." The rest remained a mystery. Like the fact that the professor had entrusted the Grim Reaper with the book in the first place. The professor himself had left town, of course, but my dad had also met a Reaper at one point. Was it him? I debated asking, but that might get me shut down, and I had other questions which were more pertinent. "Is it true that the Reaper Council is watching Ivory Beach? I mean, did you get the impression they're likely to come here and intervene between Xavier and me?"

"No more or less likely than anywhere else," he said. "I admit that leaving town without informing my apprentice was an overreaction on my part."

Whoa. The Grim Reaper admitting to making a mistake? "And your reaction to Xavier visiting Evangeline?"

"My apprentice and I have cleared up the matter," he said. "Which leaves you, Aurora."

My heart sank a little at his words. "You mean... what? My relationship with Xavier, or to the Reapers? Because I'm confused on how strictly they apply their rules or whether it varies with each Reaper."

The room's temperature dropped, as though he'd figured out exactly what I was insinuating. "The Reaper

Council has some ongoing disagreements on the extent to which we must hold ourselves apart from humanity. Nevertheless, we are a world apart. They die. We do not."

"That doesn't mean you have to force your apprentice to lead a life of solitude," I said. "I don't know what Xavier's life was like before he became a Reaper, or yours, but it's impossible to wipe it from your memories, isn't it?"

"We must do exactly that in order to do our jobs." His tone was frigid. "As for my apprentice, he has known no life other than this one. He was abandoned as an infant, left on the doorstep of Grim House, and we took him in when it became clear he'd been abandoned by his Reaper parent—and presumably his other parent too."

My mouth dropped open. Why was he telling me this? Xavier himself had gone very still at my side, but I couldn't take my eyes off the Grim Reaper.

"We later found out that his father was a Reaper, but he dropped all contact with his child and had no desire to train him," said the Grim Reaper. "His mother, meanwhile, had died giving birth to him. We do not allow children to become full Reapers, so I took Xavier on as an apprentice after he reached adulthood."

"Which was my choice." Xavier finally spoke, his voice somewhat strained. "As is my decision to stand by Rory."

The Grim Reaper studied his apprentice. "You're stubborn, and young, despite your immortality. In time, when she has aged and you have not, you may come to regret your decision."

"Then we'll take it one day at a time," Xavier said. "At least allow me that."

The Grim Reaper's gaze slid between us. "Then we have nothing more to say. You may leave."

That was it? I could hardly keep my thoughts in order after the bombshell of the Grim Reaper's revelations, but it explained why he'd been so keen to keep his apprentice close at hand if he'd practically raised him single-handedly. In the end, though, Xavier's decisions were his own to make, and I hoped his boss would respect whatever route he took.

"Xavier…" I glanced at him as the door closed behind us. "I'm sorry. If you didn't want him to tell me any of that, I mean."

"I wanted to tell you myself," he said. "I hardly expected him to beat me to it. Maybe it's easier this way, though."

"You don't have to dance around the Reapers' rules, I guess." I walked alongside him through the graveyard, my mind still reeling. "Did he give us the go-ahead to keep dating, then?"

"Yes," he said. "He's right that the Reaper Council's members vary in how they apply the laws. Some don't talk to humans at all. Others may intervene in situations which would otherwise be deemed inappropriate."

"Like warning them if they're in danger of death," I said. "The thing is, *not* interfering in those situations is a choice too."

He gave a nod. "True."

"Like with my dad," I said. "He met a Reaper himself around the same time as he got entangled with the vampires. The Reaper tried to warn him from angering them by buying the book they were searching for, but he didn't listen. Then, when it was too late for him to turn back, the Reaper helped him hide the book with the professor in order to prevent the Founders from finding it."

Xavier came to a faltering stop, wonder flitting across his face. "Really?"

"Really."

"Wow." He shook his head. "I'll definitely need a while to think on that one. Want to go to the Black Dog so you can tell me all about it?"

"Sure," I said. "And you can come back to the library with me afterwards if you like. I figured out how to owl-proof my room."

His eyes widened a fraction as my words sank in. Then he grinned. "If you're sure."

"I am." Whatever came next for the two of us, I had no doubts that I wanted to face it at his side.

Xavier slid his hand into mine, and we walked away from the darkness together.

ABOUT THE AUTHOR

Elle Adams lives in the middle of England, where she spends most of her time reading an ever-growing mountain of books, planning her next adventure, or writing. Elle's books are humorous mysteries with a paranormal twist, packed with magical mayhem.

She also writes urban and contemporary fantasy novels as Emma L. Adams.

Visit http://www.elleadamsauthor.com/ to find out more about Elle's books.

Made in United States
Troutdale, OR
09/20/2024

23002254R00127